THE
DRAGON
IN THE
CORNER OFFICE

A Monstrous New York Novel

E.M. SAUBER

Editing - Tormented Author Services

Proofreading - Nice Girl, Naughty Edits

Cover Design - Impyeu

To all my badass boss babes out there, this one's for you.
Let your inner dragon soar.
Give 'em hell, darling.

NOTE FROM THE AUTHOR

Dearest reader,

Welcome to Monstrous New York! This series is set in an alternate version of New York City, where monsters and humans live together in harmony… usually. I have taken creative liberties with some of the setting, as well as Antoinette and Cyrus's occupations. So use your imagination and allow me to bend reality within the confines of these pages.

This is a sweet monster romance, but that doesn't mean we can forgo some warnings. If any of the following make you uncomfortable, please consider choosing a different book or proceed with caution.

- Parental Abandonment
- Death of a sibling (off page)
- Detailed depictions of sex between consenting adults, featuring primal play, tail play, somnophilia, and free use.
- Use of profane language

CONTENTS

CHAPTER 1

Antoinette

"That motherfucking cocksucker!" I slam the sheet of paper down on my desk. The force splinters the glass top with a sharp crack.

"Do I need the fire extinguisher again?" My assistant, Penelope, scampers into my office, perky blonde ponytail bouncing behind her.

Last week, I lost my temper and accidentally set the plant in the corner of my office on fire. Hazards of being a dragon shifter with anger issues.

Pen was able to put out the fire, and I gave her a sizable raise for her trouble. I don't know what I'd do without her. Probably burn the entire building to the ground... on accident, of course.

"No, Pen. Not this time." With a sigh, I press my fingers to my temples and massage the throbbing flesh.

Once the fire in my veins is no longer roaring, but more of a smolder, I pick up the paper again and scan the contents one more time. My worst fears are confirmed: my eyes aren't playing tricks on me. "They want me to work with that smug asshole! I can't believe it!"

Pen bounces on her toes, blue eyes peering over the top of the letter. "Work with who? The only person you get this worked up over is—"

"Cyrus Wilcox." Plumes of smoke billow from my nostrils, the flames in my belly sparking to life once again at the ashy taste of his name on my tongue.

Before my exhaled breath can incinerate the paper, Pen plucks it from my hands. Her eyes sweep over each line as she mumbles under her breath. "A merger? 'Ms. Bauer, we are excited to inform you of the upcoming merger between York Properties and Big Apple Real Estate. During this period of adjustment, you will be assigned to partner with Big Apple's number one commercial broker, Cyrus Wilcox. We understand this is a difficult transition for everyone, and your utmost cooperation is appreciated.'"

"'Utmost cooperation,' my ass. They can't do this to me! I've been the top performing commercial broker for over five years!" Thick smoke swirls in the air around me as my chest heaves, the stiff fabric of my designer blazer straining with each labored breath.

Hooking a thumb over her shoulder while backing up a few steps, Pen murmurs, "I'm gonna get the fire extinguisher. Deep breaths, Annie."

Taking her advice, I let my eyes fall closed and focus on anything besides Cyrus Wilcox's smug face. With his perfectly coiffed dark-blonde hair and stupid sparkling blue eyes. Ugh. His suits always fit his thickly muscled frame like they've been sewn on.

Wouldn't put it past him. The man must spend hours getting ready every morning.

There's no way a human male looks *that* perfect without a lot of help.

"Annie, you're doing it again..."

Sure enough, when my eyes spring open, a small flame flickers on the discarded notebook in the center of my desk. "Shit!" Using my hand, I smack it over the flame until it's extinguished and my palm is tinted black from the soot.

Another perk of being a dragon shifter: fire doesn't burn me.

Whooshing a breath from my lungs, I expel any thoughts of a certain blonde-haired nemesis from my body. "Sorry, sorry. I'm calm. I swear."

"Good. Let's keep it that way. The memo says there's a meeting with Mr. Andrews and Cyrus this afternoon to discuss moving into a shared office... immediately." Pen's pert nose scrunches as she peers up at me. "I guess you'll have to bump your daily yoga session to twice a day to keep your anger in check."

The damn throbbing starts in my temples again. *You'll be fine. He's just a man. A human.*

For the past fifty years, monsters and humans have learned to live in harmony. New York City being the heart of monster society. And I get along with everyone, except Cyrus Wilcox.

My heels click on the tile floor as I enter the CEO's office, eyes narrowed on the man who's hell-bent on making my job harder.

Pen trails behind me, notebook tucked under her arm. I cross the office and take a seat next to the bane of my existence: Cyrus Wilcox.

"Ms. Bauer," he drawls. The crisp baritone of his voice grates on my nerves, but sparks an uncomfortable heat in my core that I choose to ignore. "You're looking lovely this morning."

I bite my tongue to hold back my scathing remark about commenting on a woman's appearance, and settle on,

"Good morning, Wilcox. Unfortunately, it looks like we'll be seeing a lot more of each other."

Seated behind the desk in front of us, Mr. Andrews, the owner of York Properties, clears his throat. "Ms. Bauer, thank you for joining us. Now that you're both here, let's get started. Cyrus, thank you for meeting in person. I know you're a busy man."

Somehow, I hold in my scoff. Apparently, I'm *not* busy? My calendar full of client meetings and property walk-throughs would prove otherwise.

Cyrus chuckles, leaning back in his chair and crossing one ankle over his knee. "Not a problem, Robert. Doesn't hurt that my office is right next door." His crystalline eyes swing to the wall of windows behind me, specifically the skyscraper where Big Apple takes up residence. For now, at least.

"Right," Mr. Andrews continues. "My brother and I have finally repaired our once tumultuous relationship and decided to merge York Properties and Big Apple. I'll be spearheading the operation, acting as CEO, while he maintains a more hands-off approach, continuing to work remotely. We've decided the new company, Big York Properties, will remain in this building." He taps one thick finger against his desk. At least I won't have to move to a new building—silver lining. "You're our top performing agents, so it's a no-brainer to keep you both on payroll. However, rather than working independently, we want you working as a team. Learn from each other and take our company to the next level."

I bristle, digging my nails into the palms of my hands to keep my temper at bay. "And that requires sharing an office?" Raising my chin, the clear, nictitating membrane in my eyes shuts and opens quickly. I don't waiver an inch as Mr. Andrews's beady eyes skim me from head to toe, making my skin crawl.

I've never liked him, but he offered me a job ten years ago when I was down on my luck—thanks to Cyrus.

Once upon a time, Cyrus and I were colleagues at Big Apple until he fucked me over. We were gunning for the same sale and he undercut my offer to the client, which led to me getting fired.

York Properties took a risk, offering me a job when I needed it most. I've worked my ass off since then, and clawed my way back to the top.

"Truth be told, we're renovating during the rebrand and there's only one office available. So if you'd rather work in a supply closet, be my guest." His tone is demeaning, but I don't shrink under his lingering gaze. Even if he is a bit sleazy, he's a smart man, and he knows he can't afford to lose me. My numbers are consistent, and I always deliver; gaining new clients each month and finding hidden real estate gems throughout the city.

"Come on, Antoinette." Cyrus's smooth voice melts over me, breaking my stare-off with my boss. This pull my body has to him... I hate it. I slice my gaze to his while he continues speaking. "Maybe you'll learn something from me." He winks, and I want to punch him. Wipe the smug smirk right off his pretentious face.

Rage simmers under my skin, and if I don't get out of here soon, I'm liable to start another fire.

"It's a corner office," Mr. Andrews says, goading me with the promise of floor-to-ceiling windows and probably a private bathroom. "One of the old VP suites. And Penelope will act as assistant to both of you going forward."

Peeking over my shoulder, I offer Pen a reassuring smile, one she returns before focusing back on her notes.

Pen's presence alone calms my temper, so maybe sharing an office with Cyrus won't be the worst thing in the world. Oh, who am I kidding? Even ten of Pen couldn't keep me calm around him. With a huff, I cross my arms over my chest and relent. "Fine."

"Good. Over the next month, find a property within the city. Ms. Bauer, I know you're good at finding those hidden diamonds no one else can. Use your skills."

The man may be a skeeze, but I sit up a little straighter under his compliment. On several occasions, his misogynistic tendencies have made me question why I still work here, but I'm so close.

I've scrimped and saved my entire working career in hopes of one day opening my own firm. My bank account and my name in the commercial real estate world are nearly ready for me to take the leap and hack it on my own.

Andrews drones on. "And plan a renovation that will wow us—but do it together. This is a joint venture, not a competition. Understood?"

Ever the brown-noser, Cyrus speaks first. "Won't be a problem, Robert. Thank you for the opportunity." He even goes so far as to shake Mr. Andrews's hand while leveling me with a shit-eating grin. Asshole.

Mr. Andrews's gaze lands on me, his thick eyebrow raised expectantly. A joint project with Cyrus could gain me the last ounce of respect I need in a male-dominated industry before starting my own firm.

Suck it up, buttercup. This is your ticket out of here.

"Yes, sir. I understand. I already have a lead on an amazing property. You won't be disappointed." My tone is as sugary and sweet as I can manage with the lava pumping under my skin.

"I knew I could count on our two best agents," Mr. Andrews says as my phone chimes in my hand.

Standing from my seat, I nod at both men. "If you'll excuse us. I have an urgent meeting with a client."

Pen follows behind as I hightail it out of the office, the beginnings of an inferno burning under my skin. Welcome to your own personal hell, Antoinette.

CHAPTER 2

Antoinette

A few days later, I ease into my new office chair, spinning to face the floor-to-ceiling windows. The sun has barely risen, casting a fiery red glow on the world. Sighing, I soak in the picturesque scene before me. Beams of light shattering around the skyscrapers of the city, creating a kaleidoscope of colors along the miles of glass.

This is my favorite time of day. Everything is fresh and new. Opportunities around every corner, ripe for the plucking.

The office is quiet and calm; it's perfect, really. I find I get my best thinking done first thing in the morning, so I always get here around six o'clock.

Seems my luck has run out today. An incessant clacking comes from my right, followed by the tapping of a pen on the desktop. My blood boils, whooshing through my ears, nearly drowning out the sounds of my new office mate.

It would seem Cyrus *also* gets his best thinking done early in the morning.

Lucky me.

Swiveling in my chair, I brace my elbows on my desk and glare at him. Stupid blonde hair and immaculately fitted navy suit. Even his fucking tie is perfectly straight and color-coordinated to his pale-burgundy dress shirt.

Our L-shaped desks are on opposite sides of the office; one in each corner along the windows. From my vantage point, I have the perfect view of his profile as he faces his computer monitor.

"Must you be so loud, Mr. Wilcox? Some of us are trying to work."

Feet braced on the floor, he spins his chair until our eyes lock. Icy blue meeting luminous gold. Like two cowboys facing off in a duel at high noon, the heavy weight of our stares is electric as they hang in the air. "I'm sorry if I've disrupted your flawless routine, Ms. Bauer. I, too, was impacted by this god-awful merger. Or did you forget?"

I shrug, not dignifying his mocking tone with a verbal response, but he forges on. "Might I suggest we form a truce for the time being and make the best of an abysmal situation?" One thick eyebrow rises in question.

I huff. "Whatever. Please keep your noises to a minimum and stay on your side of the office."

"Good." With a harsh nod, he turns back toward his computer, totally ignoring my request and clicking the end of his damn pen like he's starting a fire.

Before I can open my mouth to further berate him, Pen saunters into the office, a steaming mug of tea in her hand.

Sighing, I take the mug from her hands. "Thank you, Pen. What would I do without you?"

Bringing it to my lips, my breath ripples across the dark-brown surface as I cool the tea before taking a sip. The warm liquid slides down my throat, calming my frazzled temper. Lavender chamomile always does the trick.

She returns my smile with one of her own, perching her butt on the corner of my desk. Notebook and pen in hand, she's ready for our morning check-in.

Like me, Penelope Martin is an early bird, always ready to grab the metaphorical worm by its balls. We've made an excellent team for five years now. "For one"—she lowers her voice—"you'd murder that poor man or accidentally burn the entire building down."

Clutching at my pearl necklace, I gasp. "Well, I never."

One corner of her mouth hitches up, an adorable dimple popping into place. Pen is in her late-twenties. I took a chance on her, fresh out of business school, and not a day goes by that I regret my decision. As a centuries old dragon shifter, jaded by a lonely life, I need someone bubbly and optimistic like her to keep me sane. "You know you would."

"Fine," I relent with a subtle eye roll, but my lips tip into a small smile, making her chuckle. "What's on the schedule for today?"

At that moment, a shadow lingers over me, blocking the bright rays of sun streaming through the window behind me. "Yes, Miss Martin, what is on *our* schedule today?" His deep voice at my back has lava flowing through my veins. If I look in a mirror right now, my golden eyes will glow even brighter than usual with my hackles up.

"Mr. Wilcox, don't you have your own work to prioritize?" I grit out through clenched teeth. "Simply because we have to share this glass cage does not mean we have to actually work together. You stay on your side. I'll stay on mine." For dramatic effect, I point from his side of the office to mine.

He has the audacity to place his big mitts on the back of my chair and spin me until I'm caught in his icy gaze.

Leaning a palm on each arm of my chair, he cages me in, looming above me like he's the natural-born predator—not me. He's so close, his minty breath and masculine scent invade my senses, making my head spin. "No can do, princess. The big boss was very clear about us working *together*. In fact, I have a lead on a new property we can check out today."

Straightening, he glances over my head at Pen, whose mouth is gaping open like a fish out of water.

This insufferable man is trying to assert his dominance in *my* fucking office. That's not going to fly!

"Actually," I say, pushing to a stand, and coming nose to nose with Cyrus. I don't blink under the intensity of his stare. Someone needs to teach him who's in charge here—*me*. "Penelope and I already have an appointment regarding a very lucrative property on the outskirts of the city. We're due there at eight this morning. You're more than welcome to join us and watch how a real expert closes a sale." Turning on my red-bottomed heels, my shoulder-length black hair smacks him in the face as I shove past.

I'm not sure where I'm going, just that I need to be away from Cyrus. His spicy cologne fills my nose, causing an unwanted tingling in my core.

Without a backward glance, my stilettos click on the tile floor as I stomp out of the office, Pen hot on my heels, the glass door snicking shut behind her.

CHAPTER 3

Cyrus

My dick twitches in my pants, not quite sure if he should shrivel and cower under the ire of this woman. Or stand at attention and salute the lady balls she's sporting between her luscious, thick thighs.

An aroma of smoke and lavender swirls around me as Antoinette retreats from our first battle in our new home. One of many to come, I'm sure. The smell is just like her: intoxicating and strong.

Through the glass door of the office, her wide hips sway like a metronome as she stomps away on her skyscraper heels. Penelope trails behind like an obedient little puppy.

I knew this merger would be a nightmare, working side by side with the woman who's been my competition for the last decade.

One thing's for sure; Antoinette Bauer will chew you up and spit you out, but you'll come crawling back to be the second course. She's as fiery and unpredictable as a volcano poised to erupt. No wonder she's a dragon shifter; there's literal fire pumping through her veins.

If she wasn't such a frigid bitch, I'd totally hit that. I'm not opposed to mixing business with pleasure, especially for a woman like her: driven and hardworking, qualities I appreciate in a partner.

Plus, she's downright beautiful, with the warm hue of her olive complexion amplified by the glittering gold in her irises. The unnatural shade and vertical slit of her pupils are the only outward hints of the dragon hidden beneath her skin. Shiny black hair cut into a severe line brushes the tops of her shoulders. It's the perfect length to wrap my fists in as I...

Clearing my throat, I spin in my chair and try to distract myself from Antoinette by counting windows on the skyscraper next door, but it's no use. My mind flies back to her like a boomerang; no amount of distraction techniques ever work.

Because did I mention her body is the stuff of wet dreams? She's built for sin. Reminiscent of a fifties pinup girl, Antoinette has the quintessential hourglass figure that drives most men wild—myself included. Mile long legs that make my mouth water are only accentuated by her tight pencil skirts and killer heels.

What I wouldn't give to let my hands follow the roadmap of every dip and valley, from her ample breasts, to her narrow waist, to her round hips and ass. There's plenty of extra cushion for when things get rough.

And I like it rough.

As much as I might find Antoinette attractive, because there's no denying it, she's been a thorn in my side for the last few years. Ever since we worked together at Big Apple, she's hated me. Something to do with her being fired after I landed a big sale on a property we were both working on. It's not my fault she's a sore loser who can't handle a little friendly competition.

Still, the way she didn't take my shit earlier has me in a tailspin between impressed, turned-on, and a little frightened.

I should have known she'd turn into a jungle cat ready to attack. Just so happened, I was the only available prey in sight.

Tucking my straining erection into the waistband of my boxers, I grunt and turn back to my computer, wiggling the mouse to wake up the screen. I simply cannot be attracted to this woman.

One: she's direct competition to my livelihood.

Two: she could literally kill me with her bare hands, which is slightly terrifying.

My cock jerks again.

What is wrong with you, Cyrus? Aroused by a woman being able to put you six-feet under?

Giving my cheek a light slap, I attempt to clear my head. Thankfully, my phone dances across the desktop, the screen lighting up with the name of one of my favorite people. The perfect distraction from Antoinette Bauer and her scarily sexy demeanor.

Shoving my earpiece in, I swipe my thumb across the screen to accept the call. "Hey, Maggie. What's up?"

There's a scuffle, then a squealed, "Uncle Cy!"

My lips pull into a smile at her excited voice. "Lily! Why are you awake so early?"

A soft giggle floats down the line. "Good morning, Uncle Cy! Guess what today is!"

I can't help but chuckle at my niece's enthusiasm at—I glance at my watch—six-thirty in the morning. Today is her fifth birthday and my sister-in-law has a special surprise planned. "Hmmm..." I tap my chin, drawing out the suspense. "Is it a very special young lady's birthday?"

Her answering squeal nearly ruptures my ear drum. "Happy birthday, Liliana Bear. I'll be there on Sunday to celebrate."

"Okay, Uncle Cy. I can't wait to see you! Did you get me a present?" I can picture her bouncing around their farmhouse right now, no doubt her mother chasing after.

"You know I did, sweetheart. I hope you have the best birthday ever today. Can I talk to your mom?"

While I wait for Lily to get her mother, I stand from my desk and pace. I do my best thinking on my feet, always have.

Wearing a path between my desk and Antoinette's, a flashing notification on her computer screen catches my eye.

She left in such a tizzy earlier; she forgot to lock her computer. *Rookie mistake, princess.*

"Hey, Cyrus. How's your new office mate?"

Placing my hand on Antoinette's computer mouse, I click the notification. "Hey, Mags. Ugh. We've already been at it this morning. The woman hates me. How am I supposed to get any work done with her eagle eyes glaring at me from across the office? It's like our boss is setting us up to fail, or worse, kill each other."

Maggie's tinkling laughter meets my ears, settling the bubbles of irritation left behind by my earlier interaction with Antoinette. "Don't be so dramatic, Cy. And don't be so hard on her. I'm sure it isn't easy for a woman of her caliber. I can imagine she's constantly judged and under-estimated in a male-dominated industry. Maybe you could learn a thing or two about patience from her."

Blowing out a sigh, I scratch the back of my neck. "I don't know, Mags. She's built me up to be the villain in her story, so why not feed into the ever-growing wedge that's already between us? A little competition never hurt anyone. Enough about me, though. What are you doing for Lily's birthday? Whatever it is, make sure you use the credit card I gave you."

"Cy, you know you don't have to take care of us. Roman made sure we don't have to worry about money in his absence." She sniffles. The mention of my younger brother has my heart clenching.

Not a day goes by that I don't miss him.

I've done everything in my power to take care of Maggie and Lily since his death, but it's not the same as him being here.

Voice quiet, I say, "I know, but I want to. It's the least I can do."

"And we appreciate it. More than you know." She's silent for a beat before continuing. "We're heading to the zoo in a few hours, so I'm sure we'll both be exhausted by the end of the day. Chasing a rambunctious four, I mean, *five*-year-old, is no joke." She laughs. "Will we see you on Sunday? Usual time?"

My lips tip into a smile. "Wouldn't miss it for the world. Have fun at the zoo and give Lil a kiss from me."

"I will. And remember what I said. You don't know the whole story, Cy. Give the woman a chance. She might surprise you."

I huff a laugh. "Doubt it. Love you, Mags. See you Sunday."

"Love you, too. Play nice." The line goes dead, and I'm left with Maggie's advice tumbling around in my brain like clothes in the dryer.

Why should I give Antoinette the benefit of the doubt? She started this feud between us. I'm all too happy to add fuel to the fire. If she thinks she can beat me at my own game, I'll show her.

Grabbing a pen, I jot the address on her computer screen down on a charred notebook sitting on her desk. "What the hell?"

Tearing the blackened piece of paper from the notebook, I swing by my desk and grab my keys before bolting out the office door. You wanna play hardball, Antoinette...? Let's fucking play!

CHAPTER 4

Antoinette

"Can you believe that man?" My voice reaches a shrill octave as Pen and I walk down the sidewalk, a cloud of smoke trailing after us.

A soft hand on my arm stops me in my tracks. Pen tugs me into our favorite diner, Cream Me Up, practically shoving my butt into a chair before plopping down across from me. "Two everythings with cream cheese, Phil. It's been a rough morning."

"Comin' right up, dollface," the shop owner calls with a wave of his green hand. Phil is a good guy, New Yorker through and through with his thick East Coast accent.

He's also an orc, which makes me feel slightly less judged for stumbling into his shop, with a plume of smoke swirling around my head. Every monster has their quirks. Mine just so happens to be a very visible indicator of my emotions.

Cream Me Up has become an unofficial safe haven for any and all monsters. Two wolven sit in the corner, sipping coffee, while a pixie flits around, delivering orders to the other patrons.

Pen draws my focus back to her with a gentle squeeze of my hand. "Annie, you cannot let him get to you, or you won't survive the rest of the week. Don't stoop to his level."

"I'm trying," I say between gritted teeth as Phil places an everything bagel in front of me. Both halves are smeared with a giant glob of cream cheese. The full-fat kind, none of that low-fat shit around here. We eat our calories and enjoy every single one of them. A mug of black coffee joins the plate as he flashes me a wink. "Thank you, Phil."

"You got it, Annie." His hulking green form retreats behind the counter and into the kitchen.

"Although... it was pretty hot how he caged you into your chair earlier." She fans herself while trapping her bottom lip between her teeth. "I could have cut the sexual tension between the two of you with a butter knife."

"Penelope Martin! We hate him. Did you forget?" Chucking a balled-up napkin at her, I level her with my best glare.

Raising her hands in surrender, she responds, "I'm just saying, what if all this animosity between the two of you could be relieved with a little *overtime?* If ya catch my drift." The dimple on her cheek pops into place as she smirks and waggles her delicate blonde eyebrows.

Cyrus's intense blue gaze flashes in my mind, and for a millisecond, I contemplate how explosive the sex between us could be. There's nothing like a good round of hate sex after some verbal sparring.

But, no! He knocked me down once and almost cost me my spot on top. No matter how scorching hot the sex would be, I can't forgive his indiscretions. "Out of the question, Pen. The man is an ass. For now, let's focus on getting this warehouse sale and impressing the board. Hopefully, they'll come to their senses and realize who the better broker is." I point a finger at myself and take a much-needed bite of my bagel.

"I thought Andrews said this wasn't a competition?"

I can't hold back the huffed laugh. "Everything is a competition when it comes to Cyrus. That's just how we work."

"Whatever you say, Annie."

Around a mouth of doughy goodness, I mumble, "Let's enjoy our breakfast without giving Cyrus Wilcox another ounce of our thoughts. Then we'll catch the train to the outskirts of the city. Mr. O'Malley is expecting us at eight."

"**T**his is the place?" Eyebrows scrunched together, Pen swings the upside-down nine in the building number back into place before pulling her finger away to glare at the black smudge left behind.

Checking my email, in the attached pictures, the place doesn't look quite as... dilapidated. Swinging my gaze between my phone screen and the dirt-crusted address marker, it matches. "Appears so."

"Aye, Miss Bauer. Is that you, lass?" The door creaks open to reveal a hunched older gentleman with a shock of white hair and thick caterpillar eyebrows. They're so thick, in fact, his crinkled eyes are barely visible.

Extending my hand, I grip his firmly in a shake. Something I learned early on in the male-dominated corporate world was to have a strong handshake. It's gotten me far in my career and earned me the respect of many colleagues and clients. "Mr. O'Malley. I'm Antoinette Bauer. It's a pleasure to meet you. This is my assistant, Penelope Martin. Thank you for meeting us this morning. Would you care to give us a tour and tell us about the place?"

He nods as we follow him inside, the double doors swinging shut and blocking out the morning sun.

Once my eyes adjust to the change in light, I spin in a slow circle as Mr. O'Malley explains the history of the building. Light streams through the upper windows and a few holes in the ceiling, illuminating the empty space.

It's wide open, and the perfect blank canvas for my vision. Sure, it needs some TLC, but the bones are here and the location is prime: close enough to the city to commute on a daily basis, but far enough into the suburbs to avoid the city noise.

The ideal bridge between suburban and urban.

I just have to convince my boss that expanding outside the heart of the city is worth his investment. Money talks, more than anything else, in his world.

"I bought this building when I was a young lad and first moved to America in the seventies. Brought the family business with me and opened 'er as a meat processin' plant. Unfortunately, I fell on hard times and the place shut down about twenty years ago. Building's paid off, but I donna have the money or time to start 'er up again." The subtle Irish brogue of his voice echoes around the vast warehouse.

"It's perfect," I whisper, locking eyes with Pen. This is the project I've been waiting for. A chance to impress the board and show them what women are really capable of. She nods, following behind Mr. O'Malley as he leads us deeper into the warehouse. "Give me a few days to draw up the offer, and I'd be happy to take it off your hands."

A shrill whistle has me stopping mid-step and spinning toward the door. "What a dump. This is your hole in one, princess?" Cyrus strolls toward us, hands tucked in the pockets of his navy slacks, like he doesn't have a care in the world.

Princess. That name again. A fire churns in my belly, incinerating the butterflies of excitement instantly.

Turning back to Mr. O'Malley, I plaster on a pleasant smile. "I'm extremely sorry about my colleague. He's still in training and learning client-facing etiquette. I hope you won't hold his behavior against me." Making a beeline over to Cyrus, I drag him away from Pen and my client by the sleeve of his jacket, while shouting over my shoulder. "Pen, could you go over the numbers with Mr. O'Malley? I'll be back in just one minute."

Once we're outside, I release his sleeve and pace the sidewalk, trying not to let my dragon explode from my body. This suit was expensive, and I rather like it. Brushing my hands down the black peplum blazer and matching black skirt, I count my breaths.

One.
Two.
Three.
Four.
Five.

The red haze in my vision settles back to normal as I blink the nictitating membrane covering my eyes a few times. Sufficiently calmed, I slice my penetrating gaze toward Cyrus, who leans casually against the side of the building, arms crossed over his broad chest. "What the actual *fuck* was that about?" I point toward the warehouse door. "How dare you come into my meeting and undermine me in front of a potential client. This is low even for you, Cyrus."

"Princess, I'm simply here to offer my services. I only want to help." He spreads his arms wide, stepping in front of me.

"I highly doubt that. And *stop* calling me princess. It's demeaning, but I think you know that."

His responding chuckle has an involuntary shiver rippling down my spine. The sound is smooth and rich, and for some reason, I like it.

No! I hate him.

"If I wanted your help, I would have asked. So, butt out!" My shoulder bumps his hard chest as I march past him. Hand poised to grasp the door handle, my motion is halted by his warm hand on my forearm.

CHAPTER 5

Cyrus

Her skin is smooth under my fingers and so much warmer than I would have expected. Is that a dragon thing? Is she always this warm?

Why does a flash of her naked in my bed, heated olive skin against mine, pop into my head? Fuck. I should let go, but I don't want to. Tugging her until our chests brush, I resist the urge to run my fingers up the sides of her neck and squeeze.

She's infuriating and bossy, all wrapped in one incredibly sexy package.

A package I should not be attracted to, but I clearly am based on the way my cock thickens in my dress pants.

Her nostrils flare and her supple breasts brush against my pecs as her chest heaves. Between the buttons of her silky blue blouse, I catch a glimpse of black lace. "Please unhand me." The breathy rasp of her voice shoots straight to my groin, but I obey, loosening my grip from her arm. Immediately, she takes a step back, removing her plush curves and intoxicating warmth from my orbit.

"Why are you here, Cyrus?"

I shrug. "If you recall, you did invite me before you stormed out of the office. I wanted to see for myself what this grand project you have planned is. And I didn't think two women should be wandering this part of the city by themselves."

Okay, that last part is a lie. Antoinette is a dragon; she's more than capable of handling herself, but maybe the chivalry will win me some brownie points.

"Excuse me?" Smoke swirls from her nostrils as an invisible breeze ruffles the sleek obsidian strands around her shoulders.

Fuck, guess that was the wrong move.

I pissed off the dragon. Again. "Mr. Wilcox, please explain what my being a *woman* has to do with my ability to conduct business. Pen and I are perfectly capable of protecting ourselves without a *man* around."

To emphasize her point further, Antoinette extends a hand between us. Except the fingers are now tipped with vicious black claws and iridescent black scales shimmer in the sun as they climb from her fingers up under the sleeve of her blazer. My throat constricts with a gulped swallow. "Okay, point made, Ms. Bauer. You win this round. Shall we continue with your meeting." Sweeping my hand toward the door, she gives a harsh nod.

"Do not underestimate me, Cyrus." Her icy tone prickles my skin when she storms past me and into the warehouse. And like the traitor he is, my damn cock twitches in my pants. *Fuck.*

"Thank you, Mr. O'Malley. We'll be in touch within the next few days with an official offer." Antoinette shakes the older gentleman's hand before following Penelope out the front door of the warehouse.

He turns to me as I extend a hand. "I owe you an apology," I say, swallowing my pride, because Antoinette is right. The way I acted earlier was totally unprofessional.

Shaking my hand, he nods, so I continue. "I'm sorry for the way I acted when I first arrived. My colleague tends to bring out the worst in me. I hope I didn't do anything to jeopardize your relationship with Ms. Bauer. I take complete responsibility for my actions."

Hopefully, the words are filled with enough conviction to get back in his good graces.

The old man chuckles, flashing me a toothy grin. "Oh, laddie. That woman could tear ya to pieces and spit ya out. It's not me ya owe an apology to." With a wink, he saunters out the front door.

Damnit, I know he's right. Especially after I put my foot in my mouth when she confronted me. I'm not a bad guy, but Antoinette seems to bring out this ultra-competitive side of me, and I don't like the person I become when she's around. She clouds my judgment until I do something I regret.

All those years ago, I never meant for her to get fired from Big Apple, but she kept one-upping me until all I could think about were the numbers and winning.

Sighing, I push the door open, bright morning sun spilling through as I step onto the sidewalk. My eyes swing to my truck, the only vehicle parked on this block. "I'm parked across the street," I announce, Pen and Antoinette both looking up from their phones. "Let me give you a ride back to the office. It's the least I can do for interrupting your meeting." My lips curl into a wide, hopefully warm and endearing grin.

Antoinette's eyes narrow on me, laced with suspicion, before she nods, following me across the street to my blacked-out truck.

"It's not practical to have a truck this big in the city," she points out as we pile into the extended cab.

Not wanting to tell her about my personal life, I keep my answer vague. "I need to haul things from time to time." Truth is, I help Mags on Sundays with house projects, and sometimes that requires a truck.

Clearly not liking my answer, Antoinette huffs and crosses her arms over her chest. The action pushes the swells of her breasts together, a deep valley forming between them visible in the open neckline of her blouse. What I'd give to get my hands on those juicy tits—*Nope, not gonna happen. She hates you.*

Peeling my tongue off the floor, I focus on the road ahead and getting us safely back to the office. "Look, I'm sorry for my behavior earlier. I'll admit it was less than professional." The words taste bitter on my tongue and the leather steering wheel creaks under my tight grip, knuckles turning white.

From the passenger seat, she hums, like she's deciding whether to boot me out the driver's side door or not. "I guess I'll accept your apology. This project could be huge for the company, so I would appreciate your cooperation." Her tone is clipped, those golden eyes fixed on the passing buildings out her window.

Glancing in the rearview mirror, Penelope's gaze is glued to her phone.

Clearing my throat, I try to engage Antoinette in conversation. "What's your plan with the warehouse? I thought York and Big Apple were only interested in downtown properties?"

I'll admit, this property is further out of the city than I would have chosen, but Antoinette must have an angle. She's savvy and smart when it comes to commercial real estate.

Her fingers curl around the seatbelt where it lays across her chest, eyes closing on a hum. "They are. I'm hoping to change their minds."

"How?"

She laughs, the sound melodic and soothing. Damn, she has a great laugh. Too bad she uses it so sparingly. "You expect me to spill all my secrets, Mr. Wilcox?" Betraying me, my cock jerks at her use of my formal name again.

"Come on, Antoinette." My gaze flashes to hers before returning to the city streets ahead. "If we have to work together, a certain amount of trust is required, right?"

"Trust you haven't earned."

"*Yet*," I say, flashing her a wink. I don't miss the slight flush that creeps across her cheeks before she huffs and turns her attention out the passenger window again, effectively ending our conversation.

The rest of the ride passes in silence. Thankfully, it's short since traffic moves smoothly.

As soon as I pull into my assigned parking spot in the underground ramp, Antoinette and Penelope are out of the truck like it's on fire.

Turning off the engine, I run a hand over my chin, the coarse five o'clock shadow rasping against my palm. This is only the first day and we've already had two spats. How am I going to survive this indefinitely?

Chapter 6

Cyrus

Fortunately, the rest of the week passes relatively smoothly between me and Antoinette. We only had a minor incident when I didn't replace the paper in the shared printer in our office.

The casualty was the poor potted plant on the corner of Antoinette's desk.

She burned it to a crisp in her hissy fit. Overreact much?

Because I'm a nice guy, I plan to buy a replacement before Monday.

It's Sunday and the truck windows are rolled down as I cruise along the country road to my sister-in-law's house.

A light breeze ruffles the strands of my hair, and the clean air has all the animosity from the past week melting from my body.

Maggie and Lily live about an hour north of New York City in an old farmhouse. Roman, my brother, had grand plans to fix it up, but he never got that far.

Since his death, those plans have fallen on my shoulders, since I know Mags doesn't have the heart to sell the property. In all honesty, I don't mind coming here every weekend and doing a little manual labor. It's good for my body and gives me a chance to spend time with my niece.

Pulling off the paved road, gravel crunches under my tires, and the truck bounces on the uneven dirt of the long driveway leading to their house. The box in the passenger seat rattles and shifts with each bump in the road. The obnoxious rainbow foil wrapping paper sends a treasure trove of colors flashing around the truck's cab.

Lily is in a hardcore rainbow phase, so when I saw the wrapping paper at the store, I knew it was perfect for her.

Apple trees line the road as I approach their house, a worn wooden fence separating the property from the gravel road.

Finally, the white two-story farmhouse comes into view, black shutters on every window and a wooden porch wrapping around the whole thing. I spent most weekends last summer fixing all the holes in the deck and adding a fresh coat of stain. Combined with the outdoor furniture and the plants Maggie added, the place is warm and welcoming.

As my truck rolls to a stop, the cherry red front door bangs open, a little girl barreling out of the house. "Uncle Cyrus! You're here! Momma, he's here!"

I can't help but laugh at her enthusiasm, her curly pigtails bouncing with each step. This little girl has kept me grounded, and she doesn't even know it.

Lily was barely one when Roman died, so she doesn't really remember him.

Before his death, I was too much of an asshole, too full of myself to spend much time with my brother and his family. Maybe part of me was jealous because he was living domestic bliss, something I wasn't even sure I wanted.

But at thirty-eight, I'm starting to realize kids aren't in the cards for me, so I'll spoil Lily rotten.

"Liliana Bear!" Throwing the truck in park, I hop out and spread my arms in the nick of time to catch her as she launches her tiny body at me. "How's my birthday girl?" I ask, smacking a kiss on her cheek before blowing a raspberry under her chin.

The cutest giggle echoes through the air as she uses her little hands to pry me away. "That tickles and your face is scratchy!"

On the weekends, I give my skin a break from shaving daily and let the stubble grow out until Monday morning. I rub the offending hair against her cheek, sending her into another fit of laughter. A creak from the porch has me pulling back. Still clutching Lily in my arms, my gaze lands on Maggie.

Lily is the spitting image of her mother; curly blonde hair, skin decorated with freckles, and beautiful green eyes like sea glass.

Maggie's lips pull into a grin, revealing the slight gap between her front teeth. Even at thirty-five, she still has girl-next-door good looks. Innocent and sweet, to match her kind personality. She's always been like a little sister to me.

"Hey, stranger. How've you been?" she asks in greeting. Smiling, she crosses her arms and leans against the open door.

Hoisting Lily up until she's situated on my shoulders, I climb the porch steps and pull Mags into a side hug. "Better now. This place always takes away the stress of the week. Are we ready to celebrate someone's birthday?"

Lily squeals and kicks her bare feet against my shoulders. It's early September, so the air is still warm with the last remnants of summer.

"Oh! I brought a cake and a present. They're in the truck cab. Can you grab them, Maggie?"

She takes my keys from my outstretched hand and bounds toward the truck as I go inside, careful to duck through the doorway so Lily doesn't hit her head on the doorframe. "How was the zoo, Liliana Bear?"

While I find my way to the living room, Lily rambles on about all the animals she saw on their trip to the zoo. "It was so fun, Uncle Cy! We saw an... an... Momma, what was the scaly rat thing called again?"

Maggie enters the room with an arm full, setting the cake and rainbow-covered gift on the coffee table. "An armadillo, Lily bug."

"An armadillo! It was so awesome!" she squawks as I swing her from my shoulders and plop her on the couch. Her cheeks are flushed a rosy hue and the excitement in her sweet voice has warmth pumping from my heart to the tips of my fingers and toes. Maggie's eyes twinkle as they linger on Lily, a soft smile tipping up one corner of her mouth.

This is exactly what I needed after a week of sparring with Antoinette Bauer.

A few hours later, we're sitting around the kitchen table, about to cut into the cake I brought. A giant rainbow arches across the top, with five candles scattered around the edges. The small flames flicker in the late afternoon light. "Happy birthday to you!" As we sing the final note, Lily sucks in a huge breath, little chest puffed to full capacity.

"Blow 'em out, Lily girl!" Mags encourages.

A gusted breath leaves Lily, spittle flying onto the candles... and the cake. After a few more attempts, the final candle flickers out and my phone vibrates incessantly in my pocket.

Shoving my hand into the pocket of my jeans, I pull it out. The name on the screen has my temperature rising, and not in a good way. *Why is she calling me on a Sunday?*

Standing from the table, I hold up the offending phone and say, "Excuse me a second. I need to take this call quick."

Maggie nods, already cutting into the cake while Lily bounces in her seat.

Stepping into the kitchen, I lean against the counter with a sigh, thumb swiping over to accept the call. "Yes, Ms. Bauer," I answer, words laced with annoyance that I hope she notices.

Shuffling of papers filters down the line, followed by an irritated huff. "Have you seen the contract for the O'Malley property? I left it on your desk on Friday for your final review, and now I can't find it. We need to get the numbers finalized and get the project off the ground—"

"Antoinette."

"If we don't get this contract finalized"—more shuffling papers—"we could lose the sale."

"Antoinette." She's spiraling. I can practically picture the smoke billowing from her flared nostrils while her hands are buried in a pile of paperwork.

I've never met someone with a temper like Antoinette. Her fuse is almost non-existent. It would be funny how fast she flies into a tizzy if I wasn't worried she'd set the whole damn office on fire.

"Hmm." Finally the rustling stops and a sigh whooshes to my ear.

"Breathe for me. Can you do that? Match my breathing." I blow out a long breath, listening for her to do the same. When she does, I suck in a long inhale, filling my lungs until they might burst. We repeat this process a few more times until I'm sure she's calm. "Good girl. The contract is in my briefcase... at home. Do *not* panic. I looked over everything last night, and it's ready for Penelope to send to O'Malley in the morning. Okay?"

The line is silent for a second, then her raspy voice hits my ear. "Okay. Thank you, Cyrus."

Did she just... *thank me*?

I want to gloat and rub it in, but she's on the verge of a spiral, so I think better of it. "You're welcome, Antoinette. Now, please go home and relax. It's the weekend, for crying out loud. And please don't call me on a Sunday again. This is the one day I dedicate to spending with my family. I do not wish to be disturbed. I'll see you tomorrow."

Not giving her a chance to respond, or ask questions, I end the call and return to the dining room. From my spot in the doorway, Lily has rainbow frosting smeared on most of her face while Mags laughs behind her hand, a napkin clutched in the other hand.

My heart warms and my lips pull into a smile as Lily's giggle fills my ears and Maggie's green gaze meets mine.

This, right here, is why I work my ass off in the city during the week. Sundays are my favorite day.

CHAPTER 7

Antoinette

*T*his is the one day I dedicate to spending with my family. Cyrus's words echo in my brain as I climb the stairs to the roof. He's never mentioned a family before. Is he married?

Why do I care?

Does he have kids?

His rude and egotistical aura doesn't allude to a wife or children.

For some reason, the thought of Cyrus having a wife sends waves of jealousy roiling in my gut. The green envy monster swirls around me as I push through the roof access door and strip my clothes.

Combined with the anxiety and anger from earlier, my emotions are out of control and my dragon is clawing at my skin. She wants out—*now*.

As much as I loathe to admit it, Cyrus is right. I think I nearly barfed in my mouth admitting that, but I need to get out of the office. A flight over the city is exactly what I need to calm myself—and my dragon.

Once I'm naked and my clothes are stuffed into my black leather tote, I close my eyes and reach inward. Liquid gold eyes flash behind my lids. Iridescent black scales shift as a tail uncoils from around my dragon's massive body.

My body temperature skyrockets until fire fills my veins and explodes outward.

Bursting from the flames, my dragon tears through my subconscious and replaces my human form. I unfurl my wings and flap them through the air, creating a wind tunnel around me. Slapping my tail on the ground, I tip my head back with a roar.

In this form, I'm the size of a small compact car.

My scales ripple in the late day sunshine as the transformation completes. Damn, it feels good to be in this form. Stretching, a hoarse groan rips from my throat, muscles flexing.

It will feel even better to be soaring through the sky with the air rushing around me.

Weightless.

Insignificant.

If only to escape the suffocating confines of my mind for a moment.

To just *be*.

Clutching the handles of my tote bag with my front foot, I use my powerful back legs to press off the ground and rocket into the air above New York City. The wind whips around me, whistling in my ears and sending a bone-deep chill through my body. It extinguishes the earlier rage and jealousy I was feeling.

Down below, the buildings shrink until they're mere pinpoints on a map. This, soaring above the world and observing from afar, never gets old.

Although sometimes it does get lonely. On days like today, I wish I had someone to share it with. Someone to show the beauty of the world to as the sun reflects off the rippling surface of the ocean, like a mirror into its soul.

My wings beat faster as I approach the Statue of Liberty, her blue-green coppery facade gleaming in the evening light. Touching down between the spikes of her crown, my claws dig into the metal as I land in a crouch.

I've been coming here for years now, when I need to clear my head. Something about the boats speeding by in the harbor and the chatter of the tourists down below, some pointing as they spot me, makes me forget about any racing thoughts.

When I'm here, I don't have to be the cut-throat businesswoman.

I don't have to hide behind the carefully curated hardened persona.

I can simply exist and let the world move around me.

A few hours later, I've almost turned to stone from sitting still for so long. My scales are warm to the touch, having soaked in the last rays of the sun. The sky has turned to vibrant reds and purples as the golden globe sinks into the horizon. A rumbling in my belly tells me it's time to head home, eat, and prepare for another day of battle with Cyrus tomorrow.

The sheer curtains twist and turn in the breeze as I come in for a landing on the expansive balcony outside my penthouse. Thankfully, I remembered to leave the wide glass doors open when I left for the office in the early hours this morning. Usually, I'd take the subway or walk the few blocks home, but I needed to stretch my wings today.

I tuck my wings around my body and burst through the flames as I return to human form, strolling into my apartment with my tote bag in hand.

Working so closely with Cyrus has my thoughts in such a mess.

On the one hand, I'm still infuriated over what happened years ago.

On the other hand, I'm utterly confused. His presence stirs this strange arousal in me that I'm not sure I like. I should not be turned on by his commanding business presence, or the way his broad back stretches his suit jackets within an inch of their life.

On Friday, I found myself daydreaming like some vapid high school girl, my eyes glued to his forearms as he rolled up his sleeves. Each time he meticulously creased the cotton material before rolling it again, my pussy leaked more and more.

Of course, Cyrus was totally oblivious to the whole pornographic display, too busy schmoozing a potential client on the phone as he paced between our desks.

Luckily, Pen broke me out of my lust-filled haze when she delivered our lunches.

"Ridiculous, Antoinette. You're being ridiculous. He's just a man," I chastise myself as I trudge to the kitchen.

Popping the lid off a pre-made meal from the fridge, I set it in the microwave and punch the buttons for my desired time. While my food heats, I wander to my bedroom in search of my favorite silk robe.

The silence is deafening as my footsteps echo on the luxurious tile flooring. Today is one of those days where loneliness eats away at my soul. I've been alive for almost 200 years, living on my own for most of them, and it shows. Nowhere in my apartment is there a single picture of me with friends or family.

Not only has Cyrus one-upped me constantly in my professional life, but now he's done it in my personal life, too. He has a family who he *wants* to spend time with.

Am I jealous because I want what he has? Or because I want *him*?

Before I can spiral further, the microwave timer beeps in the kitchen. Snatching the silky black robe from my closet, I wrap the soft material around my body and breathe a sigh. This is the life I've worked my ass off for. I'm wealthy, beautiful, and independent—this is everything I've wanted since I left home at eighteen.

Right?

Grabbing my food from the microwave and a fork from the drawer, I decide to watch some trashy television to take my mind off my woes. Pen has been raving about some reality show where a man dates multiple women at once, then eliminates them one by one until he marries one of them.

Roses are involved for some reason. Humans are weird.

Not really my cup of tea, but I need a distraction from my own life right now.

I swing by my glass wine cellar, located between the kitchen and living room, to select a bottle to drown my sorrows. My hand wraps around the neck of a vintage Cabernet Sauvignon, pulling it from the rack before continuing to my favorite seat in the living room—the corner seat of my plush cream sectional that's closest to the window.

The sun has finally set, stars twinkling in the distance as I flip on the television. Bringing out one of my black claws, I slice off the paper label on the wine bottle before stabbing the cork and pulling it free, flinging it onto the coffee table. The first guzzle of the dark, sweet liquid dulls my emotions so I can settle against the couch and forget about the past week.

I need to keep Cyrus firmly in the box I've shoved him in for the past decade. He's a work rival, not a friend. And certainly not someone to get involved with in a sexual nature. No matter how alluring his twinkling blue eyes are or how much I want to mess up his perfectly styled dirty-blonde locks with my claws. Things need to remain professional. It's for the best.

It's a good thing dragons burn hot and metabolize alcohol faster than humans because I went through three bottles of wine last night while binging trashy reality television. But when I woke up this morning, my brain was blissfully numb. No thoughts of a certain irritating coworker in sight.

Shoving my bag into the gym locker, the hinges squeal as I slam it shut and lock it. It's a new week, and I'm determined to keep Cyrus from getting under my skin, so yoga first thing in the morning is a must.

One of the perks of working for a prestigious company in New York City: they have their own private gym. I've made it a habit to get a training session in most mornings before starting work.

Using up any excess energy buzzing under my skin helps keep my temper at bay and my dragon content.

Standing in front of the mirror, I slip the hair tie from my wrist and gather my sleek black strands into a high ponytail, securing it with the elastic band. You'd never know the woman in the mirror wallowed in self pity last night. No, we're done having a pity party.

"You're the boss, Annie. Don't let him get to you," I say to my reflection, glowing golden irises staring back at me, olive skin still slightly flushed from last night's wine.

Impenetrable walls back in place, I tighten the straps of my sports bra, grab my rolled-up yoga mat, and head to the gym.

CHAPTER 8

Cyrus

F^{*uck me.*}

I thought the weekend away from the office and, more importantly, away from Antoinette, was enough to squelch this annoying attraction to her.

Boy, was I wrong.

My cock jerks to life and I have to slow the speed on the treadmill as she saunters into the corporate gym on the fortieth floor.

Black leggings cling to the flare of her hips like a second skin. Unconsciously, my eyes wander to the mirrored wall behind her, lingering on the way the material stretches around each round globe of her ass. Each cheek is definitely more than a handful, mouthwatering dimples visible through the tight fabric.

I'm an ass man. Self-proclaimed, of course.

And Antoinette Bauer has an ass sailors would cross a stormy sea to bear witness to. It's a thing of beauty.

Pulling my gaze from the subtle bounce and sway of her backside, my attention is drawn to the neon purple strappy contraption holding in her ample breasts. How the fuck did she even get into that thing? And more importantly, how do I get it off her?

No, we're not attracted to this fiery woman. She hates you and probably wishes you were never born... *remember?*

As she comes to a stop next to the treadmill, my gaze lingers on the cleavage visible over the low neckline of her sports bra. With a sweaty palm, I hit the emergency stop button, and the belt slows. My sneakers squeak to a halt before I trip over my damn tongue.

"Good morning, Ms. Bauer. Did you take my advice and relax yesterday?" Still panting from my run, my voice is raspier than usual, and I don't miss the slight shiver when it rattles Antoinette's delicate, yet toned shoulders.

Her perfectly arched dark eyebrows pull together before she pinches her eyes shut and blows out a breath, fingers digging into the foam of her yoga mat. Lips moving rapidly, she murmurs something to herself.

Okay.

Right as I'm about to say her name again, her lids spring open, revealing vertical slit pupils surrounded by metallic irises that glow brighter than the sun. If I'm not careful, those eyes will hypnotize me into doing some very bad things.

Very bad things, indeed.

Her lips pull into a tight smile, those dainty fingers clutching her yoga mat. "Good morning, Mr. Wilcox. I did. And I apologize for disturbing you yesterday. I hope your wife forgives me."

Wife. One eyebrow arches at the word. "Wife? I'm not married."

A look of almost elation flits across her face, and her rigid posture softens slightly. "My mistake. I assumed you were married when you said you spend Sunday with your family."

A barked laugh breaks free from my mouth, the sound bouncing around the quiet gym. "You thought I was married. I can assure you, Antoinette, I'm on the same sinking ship as you—married to my job."

Her plump pink lips form a perfect O that has my heart rate picking up speed.

And my cock doing the thinking as I imagine shoving the thick shaft into the hollow space between those perfect lips.

Until her teeth clack together and the muscle in her jaw ticks. "Again, my mistake. Enjoy the rest of your workout." The dismissal in her clipped tone is obvious, made even more apparent as she spins in her flip-flop sandals and retreats to the other end of the gym.

Unrolling her yoga mat, she mutters under her breath as she fiddles with her phone and begins her yoga flow. At this point, I'm too confused—and oddly aroused—to focus on anything besides her, so I turn the treadmill to a low speed and walk. The whole time, my eyes remain glued to Antoinette's body. She bends and dips in every possible contortionist position, which only increases the blood flow to my groin.

She actually thought I was married. I shake my head and one corner of my mouth curves into a smile. In what world would I have time for a spouse or kids? I'm at the office before the sun rises most mornings, not leaving until it's already set most nights.

One thing I admire about the woman is the work ethic and drive we seem to share. Although, it's a double-edged sword. I'm in my late thirties and I'm utterly alone, besides Maggie and Lily.

Antoinette's misjudgment brings a nagging pain to the surface... Do I want a spouse? A partner to share my life with?

I rub at the spot over my heart, attempting to ease the uncomfortable tightness in my chest.

For some reason, my eyes wander back to Antoinette. She has all the qualities I *would* want in a partner: independent, motivated, hardworking, intelligent, financially stable, and gorgeous.

The only problem is this constant need for competition between us.

Sweat drips down my neck, soaking into the thin, athletic shirt I have on. The fabric clinging to my drenched skin has nausea rising in my stomach, so I grip the shirt at the back of my neck and pull it off. More salty perspiration cascades down my now exposed chest as I mop my skin with the shirt.

A squeak from across the gym has my head whipping up, only to lock onto a pair of luminous, fire-filled eyes.

As our gazes connect, Antoinette's normally olive skin flushes a beautiful pink.

Caught you, princess.

My mouth tips into a crooked smirk. Chuckling, I run the wadded-up shirt down my glistening abs, chasing a trail of sweat. She doesn't even blink as her eyes follow my hand. Smoke puffs out of her pert nose, something I've only witnessed when she's angry.

Right now, she looks anything but angry, skin flushed and chest heaving, pushing those tantalizing tits against the confines of her bra.

As soon as my hand reaches the waist of my athletic shorts, tugging them down ever-so-slightly, Antoinette huffs a breath, then scrambles to grab her mat and phone before stomping past me. "Asshole."

My booming laughter fills the sweat-slicked air as the door slams shut behind her. "Oh, princess. It's on."

She's attracted to me, and it's clear she doesn't want to be. I'm about to push her to her breaking point, because I can barely remember what started this damn war between us, but I'm going to be the one to end it—whether she likes it or not.

By the time I've showered and dressed—and beaten my aching cock into submission—Antoinette is already seated at her desk, deep in conversation with Penelope. With the O'Malley contract clutched in one hand, I tuck my free hand into the pocket of my gray slacks, loafers clicking on the tiled floor as I approach her desk.

"Good morning, ladies." I make sure to add a little extra pep to my voice and plaster a sunny smile on my face. "Ms. Bauer, I believe you were looking for these yesterday. Everything is up to my standards and ready for O'Malley's signature."

The subtle roll of her eyes has me stifling a laugh. Oh, she fucking hates me.

"If you're free this morning, I have a lead on another property. You're welcome to join me," I offer. Tensions have been high between us, so I'll be the one to extend an olive branch. Not that she's likely to accept it.

"I can go with," Penelope offers on her way to the office door, jumping in before Antoinette can even open her mouth. Penelope's eyes swing between me and Antoinette. Finally landing on Antoinette, she continues. "You have that meeting with accounting. Remember?" Her blonde eyebrows rise so subtly; I almost miss it.

Is she trying to keep us apart? *Interesting*.

"Oh. Yes," Antoinette says, pulling up the calendar on her computer monitor.

Well, I'll be damned. There is actually a meeting scheduled in a few minutes.

Swinging her chair back toward me, I'm met by her penetrative golden gaze. "It's about the budget for the O'Malley warehouse. Nothing you need to worry about." Her face morphs into a smug expression, like she's better than me because she found this *perfect* property.

Joke's on her. "Save some money for the rest of us. I think my lead is a property the board would love to get their hands on."

Pride radiates from me when she crosses her arms over her chest and rolls her eyes once more. "Is that so?" The double membrane on her eyes closes, then opens, tamping down the irritation evident in her stare.

I smirk. "Yes. Mr. Andrews said to find a property to wow them. I'm not putting all my eggs in that shit-hole warehouse of yours. I prefer my own basket, since I'd like some of them to hatch when this is all said and done."

Oh, that pisses her off. There are flames roaring in her gorgeous eyes, and I can't tear my gaze off her, even when thick smoke begins to pour from her nostrils.

"Oh, shit," Penelope whispers, sidling up next to me with a mug in her hands. "What did you say?" Her voice is a hiss as she sets the mug on the corner of Antoinette's desk.

In the blink of an eye, she dashes out of the office, returning a moment later with a big red fire extinguisher clutched in her shaking hands. "Annie. He didn't mean it." Glaring blue eyes snap toward me, then back toward Antoinette. "Breathe for me, Annie. In and out. Nice and slow."

It's at that moment, I realize Antoinette's chest isn't moving, like she's holding her breath.

Suddenly, her chest heaves, and she sucks in a huge lungful of air. After a few more big breaths, the smoke dissipates.

She grabs the mug and chugs the contents. "Thank you, Pen," she gasps, setting the empty mug on the desktop. "At least I didn't set anything on fire this time." Her laughter is clipped, her smile forced.

"Silver lining?" Penelope shrugs. "Come on, Mr. Wilcox. Let's not add insult to injury." She nods toward the door, and I follow behind her with one last backward glance at Antoinette. Her eyes are shut, and her chest rises and falls in a steady rhythm.

Chapter 9

Cyrus

"Care to explain what happened back there?" Settling into the driver's seat of my truck, I hook a thumb over my shoulder, toward the building.

Penelope buckles her seatbelt before clasping her hands in her lap. "That, Mr. Wilcox, was a dragon shifter nearly losing her temper on you. First time?"

I choke on a laugh. "Uh... yeah. Does that happen often?"

She shrugs, wincing. "When it comes to matters involving you? Yes. Small piece of advice, Mr. Wilcox. Don't push her buttons."

"It's Cyrus." Cranking the key in the ignition, I shift into reverse and back out of the parking spot.

"What?"

Waving at the parking garage attendant, I pull onto the busy city street, horns honking around us as cars weave in and out of traffic. "You keep calling me 'Mr. Wilcox.' I don't like it. Call me Cyrus, please."

Penelope nods, hands clutching the shoulder strap of her seat belt. "Okay, Cyrus. Annie's already struggling with this merger. You don't have to make it even more difficult by being a... a dick." She coughs. "No offense."

I can't help but chuckle. I get the impression Penelope Martin doesn't curse often, so the fact I've gotten a rise out of her is amusing. "None taken. I know I can come off a little pompous, but sometimes you have to be if you want to make it in this business."

She hums, eyes straight ahead. "Annie's worked hard to get where she is. You might think she's cold and heartless, but I know better. She's an amazing boss and one of my closest friends."

Fuck. My stomach drops. Was I being an asshole on purpose earlier? Yes.

Did I have to be? Probably not.

Maggie's words come to mind again. *Don't be so hard on her. You don't know the whole story.* I realize I know virtually nothing about Antoinette Bauer. And if I want to survive the next month working together, I need to know one thing for sure. "So what's the secret?"

"Hmmm?" The ends of her perky blonde ponytail swish over her shoulders when her head jerks toward me. "Secret to what?"

"To get on Ms. Bauer's good side." The leather of the steering wheel creaks when my grip tightens. "If she has one," I add under my breath.

"I don't know if I'm comfortable getting in the middle of whatever is going on between you two."

"Look, Penelope, to tell you the truth, I'm not entirely sure what's going on between us either. Antoinette hates me for reasons beyond my understanding, but I'd like to change that to make our working conditions more desirable for *everyone.* Yourself included."

Her delicate throat ripples with a swallow and she blows out a breath, the burst of air ruffling the stray hairs framing her face. "Okay, if you think it will help."

I shrug. "It can't hurt."

"Well, she really likes lavender chamomile tea. It helps keep her temper in check. You could try making her a cup before talking to her. Especially first thing in the morning. That's when she's most volatile. Oh! And everything bagels with cream cheese are her kryptonite. Especially from Cream Me Up."

My eyebrows shoot up. "Excuse me."

Penelope giggles at what I'm sure is a look of mortification on my face. "You know the diner on 7th? It's called Cream Me Up. Phil runs it. He's an orc. Real nice guy."

I shake my head, still trying to get over the name. "I'm afraid I'm not familiar."

"I'll send you the address. And... my favorite is the blueberry with cinnamon sugar cream cheese." Long lashes lower in a wink, a cheeky smile showcasing twin dimples on her cheeks. "Since you'd be stopping anyway."

Sneaky minx. My booming laughter fills the small space of the truck cab, soon joined by Penelope's giggles. "Fair point. And noted. Anything else?"

She taps her chin, lips pursing as she thinks. "If smoke starts to come out of her nose, you better make like a magician's assistant and disappear."

I swallow around the lump in my throat, remembering the look of unhindered rage in Antoinette's eyes earlier. I've never seen them glow so bright before, like we were on the surface of the sun. In that moment, I wasn't totally sure she wouldn't burn me to a crisp. Not something I want to experience again. "Got it. I rather enjoy being alive." I flash a quick smile at Penelope before turning right to follow the river.

"*T*his is your hole in one?" In the passenger seat, Penelope turns toward me, eyes wide.

The truck crawls to a stop, and I throw it in park. "Umm, I guess the pictures were a little misleading." Climbing out of the truck, I'm met by a row of brownstones that have seen better days. The brick facade is crumbling, a pile of tan bricks scattered across the sidewalk near one corner. Vines cover most of the front, rooted deep into the mortar. "Maybe the inside is in better shape." But my stomach sinks as I say the words. The inside is almost never in better shape than the outside.

As I'm rounding the front of my truck, a flashy red sports car screeches to a stop behind my vehicle, nearly hitting my bumper. The driver's side door swings open, and my college buddy, Martin, steps out.

We met in business school, but ended up taking commercial broker jobs that took us to different parts of the city. Every now and then, he'll throw me a bone if one of his clients has a property that needs to be offloaded for cheap. Case and point: the pile of bricks in front of us.

"Get her to sign those papers. No matter what. We need this deal," he commands into the earpiece sticking out of his ear.

Ripping it from his ear, he tosses it on the seat and slams the door before turning to me with a smile plastered on his face. "Cy! Good to see you!" He grips my hand in a firm shake, but his eyes are glued to Penelope's ass as she walks away from us, inspecting the building. "Sorry I'm late. Trying to close this deal that could make me a fortune. You know how it goes."

Letting go of my hand, he bumps my shoulder, like we're old pals. We aren't. I've kept in contact with Martin simply because he finds me hidden gems on occasion. Except, as another brick tumbles off the front of the building, I'm doubting his skills. Penelope jumps out of the way of the falling debris with a shriek.

"Who's the dime? You mixing business with pleasure? Cy, you sly dog." Martin tips his head toward Pen and waggles his eyebrows. The slimy smirk on his face reminds me exactly why I keep our interactions strictly business.

"*That* is my assistant, Martin. Show her some respect. She puts up with a lot between me and Antoinette."

His smile turns even more lecherous at my words. "The dragon shifter... That's right. And how is the big, bad bitch of the west?"

Gnashing my teeth, my jaw muscles flex, and I resist the urge to knock him out. Just because there's animosity between me and Antoinette, it doesn't mean I'll allow someone to insult her.

Deep down, some latent part of me feels possessive of her. And I don't have the faintest idea why.

"Watch it, Martin." The growl in my voice doesn't seem to faze him.

He chuckles, hands raised as he backs toward the building. "Sorry, man. Didn't mean to offend anyone."

Reluctantly, I follow him and Penelope into the run-down building, my hopes of this being a diamond in the rough dropping with each step.

"My client will cut you a sweet deal if you sign the papers today. The place just needs a little love, but the bones are there." He knocks his knuckles against the drywall, scowling and brushing his hand on his pants when it comes away covered in plaster dust. Schooling his features, Martin swings his smarmy smile my way, continuing down the hall. "Plus, the location is dynamite. Can't beat being right on the river. You know Andrews and his brother can afford the rehab."

"A *little* love?" Pen winces, stepping around a patch of black mold on the water-stained hardwood floor.

Any and all confidence in Martin is obliterated when I walk into the living room. Water drips from a giant hole in the ceiling, the upstairs floorboards hanging down into the first floor.

Mouth gaping, I walk under the hole with my head tipped and sunlight meets my eyes. "This goes all the way to the roof. And with the black mold in the hallway, it's a complete gut job."

Before I can berate Martin for wasting my time, Penelope's scream fills the air. "Rats!"

Spinning on my heels, sure enough, a handful of rats scatters to the corner of the room.

I'm out.

This property is a money pit. There's no way Andrews and the board would give me the money for repairs.

Scream trailing behind her, Penelope bolts out the front door, and I'm only a few steps behind.

By the time I make it outside, Penelope is in the truck. Coming to stand next to me, Martin runs a hand over his gelled brown hair, scratching the back of his neck. "I swear I didn't know it was this bad, Cy." But his face is anything but apologetic. The man only sees dollar signs, so I'm sure that's why he tried to get me to take this place off his hands.

"Can't do it, Martin. Next time, vet the place before wasting my time."

He nods.

Feeling that I don't owe him anything else, I climb my defeated ass into my truck and head back to the office.

I guess all my eggs will have to go into Antoinette's basket. And, starting tomorrow, I'll be making daily trips to Cream Me Up to butter her up in hopes of getting on her good side.

CHAPTER 10

Antoinette

Why is he being nice to me? A steaming to-go cup of lavender chamomile tea waits on my desk when I get to the office. An everything bagel slathered in cream cheese sits on a plate to the side.

These gifts have been appearing on an almost daily basis for the past week.

A quick glance at my watch shows it's too early for Penelope to be here yet. Which leaves only one person who could be responsible for the—dare I say—*kind* gesture.

Cyrus sits at his desk, face lit up by the brightness of his computer screen. The office lights are still off, only the beginning rays of morning sun spilling in through the massive wall of windows. He's engrossed in whatever he's looking at, so I allow myself a few seconds to admire his appearance.

Admittedly, Cyrus Wilcox is an attractive man. Even I can swallow my pride and admit that.

His dark-blonde hair is gelled back to perfection like it is every day. I wonder how much product he puts in those strands to get it styled so immaculately.

My gaze skims down to his thick eyebrows, furrowed over icy-blue eyes.

Eyes that could stare straight into my soul if I'm not careful. Cyrus seems like the type of man who could get me to let down my walls, and I'm not quite ready for anyone to get inside my fortress of solitude. I've been alone for so long that I'm not sure I even know how to have a relationship of the romantic variety.

The best I can do is fuck without any attachment. And I don't even do that often.

Shaking my head, I banish the runaway thoughts because I am *not*—under any circumstances—interested in Cyrus Wilcox. Especially not in a romantic way. I just have to make it through this month and, hopefully, the board will realize it's madness to have us work as a team. Then we can part ways amicably and go back to being rivals.

But the pinpricks of lust scattering goosebumps across my skin have me doubting myself.

Dropping my tote bag on the floor under my desk, I plop into my swivel chair and get my laptop out. Cyrus still hasn't looked up from his screen, so I finish my perusal while my computer boots up. A strong nose leads to a set of pouty lips. Lips, I'm a little ashamed to admit, have been featured in my dreams at night.

I've noticed his face is always smooth and freshly shaved, and I bet it would feel amazing between my legs...

How long has it been since I last got laid?

Based on the burning between my thighs... Too long.

But I can't go there with Cyrus. He's the reason I lost my job ten years ago. He can't be the reason I lose this one, too. I can only imagine he's got something up his sleeve to one up me.

He keeps talking about this mysterious property that's on his radar.

Huffing, familiar irritation simmers under my skin, my dragon coming to life in my chest.

"Nope," I whisper. "Ignore him."

Taking a sip of my tea, I pop in my earbuds, start some calming spa music, and pull up my digital renderings for the O'Malley warehouse.

Not for the first time, I push away the deep-seated loneliness that's been rearing its ugly face more and more lately. I don't need anyone. I've made it this far on my own. All I need is my job.

It's Sunday again.

And I'm at the office... *again.*

The truth is, I have nothing better to do with my time. So I might as well get a jumpstart on the week. Right?

I thought about asking Pen if she wanted to grab brunch, but I remembered she's at a baseball game with her brother, niece, and nephew. I'm the one who bought them tickets, for crying out loud. Her brother is a huge Yankees fan, so I helped Pen get tickets for his birthday.

Plus, I can't take away from her family time, even if I'm lonely.

I really need more friends.

Shuffling through the stacks of folders on my desk, I search for the O'Malley contract. The old man still hasn't accepted my offer, which is more than generous, if I do say so myself.

And I do.

"Where the fuck is it?" In my haste, my finger snags along the edge of a paper. Pain rips through the tip when the paper slices into my skin. "Fuck," I hiss, bringing the injured finger to my mouth and sucking the blood away.

The red liquid continues to ooze from the cut while I rummage through my tote bag for a bandage. Nothing. Must have used the last one after one of my temper flare-ups.

Lifting my head, my gaze snags on the desk across the office. I wonder if Cyrus has any?

Still sucking on my bloodied finger, I creep across the office to his desk. My stomach does a little cartwheel when I run my hand over the back of his desk chair, rolling it out of the way.

Why does this feel wrong? Being in his space when he's not around.

He invaded my privacy by crashing my meeting with O'Malley. Cyrus isn't even here; he'll never notice.

And it's one little bandage.

What am I supposed to do? Drip blood all over the important documents like a heathen. No.

Huffing a sigh, I jerk open the center drawer of his desk. The small space is littered with pens and paper clips, a stack of sticky notes. Clearly, the man is unorganized. It's a wonder he's made it as far as he has in the business world.

A little white rectangle catches my eye, sticking out from under a few pens. Snatching it up, I tear open the paper and wrap the bandage around my sore finger. "Perfect."

Closing the drawer, I step back and grip the top of his desk chair, prepared to wheel it back in place so Cyrus will be none the wiser about my little theft. But my hands brush across the fabric of the suit jacket he's left draped over the chairback.

It's soft, and I can't help but curl my fists into the thick fabric and lift it to my nose. Like an addict in need of their next fix, I inhale and am immediately hit with a whiff of his cologne. Spicy and warm, with notes of—

I take another sniff.

"Mmm. Vanilla."

I'm ashamed to admit that I nuzzle my face into the fabric, letting Cyrus's distinct scent wash over every inch of my body.

It's safe.

It's soothing.

A little wave of heat zips to my core, and I clench my thighs.

No. You are not attracted to him.

Across the office, my phone chimes on my desk. Dropping the jacket onto the back of the chair, I practically skip over to my desk, excitement swirling through me.

Maybe Pen's brother canceled, and she wants to meet for brunch after all.

Grabbing my phone, I turn it over. The last name I'd expect lights up the screen.

> **Wilcox: It's a beautiful Sunday, princess. You better not be wasting it at the office.**

I whip my head up, searching every corner of the room for... I'm not sure what.

I'm utterly alone.

Just me and the poor wilting plant on my desk. Reaching out a finger, I poke at one of the floppy, yellowing leaves and wince.

He can't possibly know I'm here.

Blowing out a breath, I plop down into my chair, eyes focusing on my computer screen.

But no matter how hard I try, my gaze wanders back to the jacket hanging on Cyrus's chair. It's a reminder that, unlike me, he has a life outside of work. He probably left it behind in his haste to get out of here on Friday. His thoughts no doubt clouded by the excitement of his weekend plans.

I, on the other hand, dread the weekends. If I'm not working, then I usually spend my time doing yoga, soaring above the city, or watching too much reality television. All activities I do in solitude.

Some life I'm living.

Wasting my immortality on the mundane.

Since our little run-in at the office gym, Cyrus hasn't expanded on what family he has, but at least he has one. Besides Pen, I don't have anyone, which is why I'm here—burying myself in work—on my day off.

That all-too-familiar, and uncomfortable, black cloud of loneliness hovers over me, consuming any last bit of concentration I may have had.

"Ugh. I'll never get anything done now." Sighing, I slam my laptop shut, stuffing it and my phone into my black tote bag.

He's not even here, and he fucked up my concentration. His presence constantly lingers at the back of my mind. Why? How?

I need something to fill this void inside me before I let my feelings eat me alive. Pen may be occupied, so I'll opt for the next best thing.

Somehow, I manage not to poke my eyes out when I hastily shove my oversized sunglasses on and march out the office door.

CHAPTER 11

Antoinette

One subway ride and a few blocks later, the iconic neon pink sign for Cream Me Up comes into view. My steps quicken, and I say a little prayer of thanks that I chose to wear sensible sneakers this morning over my usual stilettos.

Carbs and caffeine are the perfect combination to lift my foul mood.

The little bell chimes happily when I push through the door, eyes searching for the big green orc who I know will put me in a better mood.

"Yo, Annie. What brings you in on a Sunday?" Phil greets me from behind the bar-height counter. His giant hand pushes a rag around the shiny lacquered top, but his deep-brown eyes are fixed on me as I huff and hoist myself onto one of the retro pink stools.

"Can't I stop by and see my favorite orc?" I perch my elbows on the clean bar top. Nestling my chin on my clasped hands, I give him a sweet smile.

Phil's booming laughter fills the quiet diner. "Last I checked, I'm the only orc you know."

Shrugging, I pick up a menu and peruse the choices, even though I order the same exact thing every time I stop by.

"Lavender chamomile and everything with cream cheese?"

My smile grows as Phil recites my usual order. "Yes, thank you. You know me so well."

Flashing a wink over his shoulder, the green giant lumbers into the kitchen to prepare my order.

Spinning on my stool, I take in the small, hole-in-the-wall diner. I stumbled upon this place a few decades ago, when monsters were newly "out," and I needed a safe space.

I love the retro vibes Phil and his wife have chosen for the decor. But they've given the place their own flare. Pink-and-white checkerboard adorns the floor, rather than the traditional black and white. Vinyl pink booths line the outer perimeter of the space, with bistro tables taking up the center. Bright purples and teals paint the walls in swirls of tye-dye.

Overhead, glowing stars, planets, and spaceships dangle from the ceiling.

It's chaotic and over the top, but I love it here.

This morning, I'm the only customer in sight, making me wonder if they're even open. My eyes flit to the sign on the door. Sure enough, the usual pink glow of the *Open* sign is noticeably absent.

"Why didn't you tell me you were closed?" I question with raised eyebrows when Phil pushes through the double doors of the kitchen.

Sliding a plate and mug in front of me, he leans his big elbows on the counter until we're eye to eye. "Looked like you could use a friend."

Guilt swirls in my stomach, making the food in front of me suddenly unappetizing. Reaching to the stool next to me, my hand wraps around the straps of my tote bag. "I can go. I'm sure you're busy and eager to get back home. I didn't mean to disturb you."

"Sit, Annie. Eat." He pushes the plate with the bagel on it closer to me.

It does look really amazing. The bagel is toasted to perfection, and a thick smear of fluffy white cream cheese is spread on each half. My stomach rumbles, reminding me I haven't eaten anything yet this morning.

Settling back in my seat, I pick up one half of the bagel and take a healthy bite. "How's Maria?" I ask once I've swallowed the doughy goodness.

My question has a broad smile lighting up his face. Two rows of white teeth glimmer in the morning sun. "Really great. She took the twins to visit her mother for the weekend." Phil is married to a pixie female. She's less than half his size, so I'm not sure how that size difference works.

His smile falters. "I got a little lonely with them being gone, so I thought I'd bake away my sorrows."

"I can relate," I admit.

"Love troubles, Annie? Maybe I can help." One black eyebrow rises as he waits for me to spill my guts.

Scoffing, I gulp down a mouthful of earthy tea. *Love?* I don't do love, and I certainly don't talk about my personal life with anyone besides Penelope, but Phil's known me for a while now. I doubt he'll judge me.

"I've been feeling extra lonely lately for some reason." I shrug, dropping my eyes to follow my finger where it drags through the thick cream cheese on my bagel.

"Have you ever thought about finding a mate? Maybe it's time to focus on something other than your career, Annie."

The familiar feeling of being unloved creeps into my body. "My mother used to tell me fairy tales of soulmates and mating bonds when I was a hatchling. But that's all they were... fairy tales. Urban legends. Dragons don't have mates, Phil." My lips curl into a tight smile before dropping to a scowl. "We live mostly in solitude once we're of age. But I've always been a little different; craving companionship more than I should."

"Then why not find a mate?"

"Is it that easy?" I ask. He found one, but I don't know anything about orc or pixie culture. Phil and his wife certainly don't seem as frosty as me. Finding love must have been easy for two cheery and upbeat individuals.

"Maria is my best friend. I can't imagine doing life without her. I'd be miserable. You just have to find someone you're willing to let in. Ya feel me?"

I swallow, but nod. That's the part of the relationship I struggle with. I'm scared to let anyone in. A cold sweat cools my normally scorching skin at the thought alone.

Phil picks up his rag again and begins cleaning the bar top around me. "What about this Cyrus guy?"

Even the mere mention of his name has my heart racing. "W-what about him?" I cough, trying to hide the quiver in my voice.

Phil shrugs. "He seems nice."

"Psh... *nice?*" I mutter before finishing the first half of my bagel.

Obviously not hearing me, Phil continues. "He's been in here every morning this week to pick up an order for you and Penelope. Couldn't you date him?"

Smoke lingers at the back of my nostrils, my hands heating as they ball into fists on the bar top. "He is the most self-centered, infuriating, obnoxious asshole of a man to walk the face of this, or any other planet in the solar system. Probably the whole galaxy."

"Bit extreme," Phil mumbles. His hand stalls mid-swipe. Eyes rising to mine, his lips curl into a smirk. "But the way you're reacting right now tells me you don't actually hate him."

"Are you high, Phil?"

He chuckles. "No, Annie. I've known you for a while now, and I've never seen anyone get you this fired up. Not even your asshole boss. Sure, you curse him out when you think I'm not listening. And I add an extra dollop of cream cheese to your bagel order."

"Bless you," I say, holding a hand to my thundering heart.

"But not even on a bad day, when you stumble in with an inferno blazing in your eyes, has your gaze burned with this..." he trails off, pointing a thick green finger at my eyes.

"With what?" I swallow, not sure I really want to know the answer. Something in my gut tells me I already know what he's going to say.

"Lust."

Fuck.

I shake my head, my low ponytail swishing along my back. "No. I refuse to give in to my attraction to *that* man!"

He hurt me before; I know he'll do it again. If he's the only choice for a partner. A mate. Whatever you choose to call it, then I'm better off alone. At least my heart would remain in one piece.

My vehement denial gets a chuckle from Phil. "If you don't want to take him as your mate, you could at least use him for some good old-fashioned hate sex. Blow off a little steam, dollface."

"Absolutely not. No way. Not happening." Draining the last of my tea, I place a pile of cash on the counter. It's definitely more than what I owe, but Phil is a staple in the monster community, so I'm willing to help where I can. "Thank you for the advice, Phil. But I'm better off shoving the man off a cliff." My lip curls into a sneer, baring one sharp fang.

"Whatever you have to tell yourself to sleep at night," Phil snarks, saluting me as I storm out of the diner. At least my belly is full now. Phil's company and the chamomile sufficiently quelled my loneliness for the time being.

Stomping back to my penthouse, I decide to spend the rest of my Sunday doing some self-care. A long soak in the tub, maybe a face mask and pedicure. Anything to build back my external armor before spending another week with Cyrus.

I'm more determined than ever to keep my interactions with him to a minimum. I'm not an idiot; I know it's inevitable since we share an office and we're forced to work on the O'Malley project together. But that doesn't mean I have to be sunshiney and sweet. He should know by now, I'm as cold as they come.

I beat Cyrus to the office the next day, lying in wait at my desk for his daily *gift*. At six on the dot, the sun is barely peeking above the horizon, and a hulking form saunters into our office. All broad shoulders and loose steps. Once again, not a hair is out of place and his solid royal blue necktie is coordinated to his paisley blue shirt.

Lips pulled into a saccharine smile that displays his perfect teeth, Cyrus prowls over to my desk with a to-go cup and pink bag in hand. The distinct pink flying saucer logo of Cream Me Up adorns both.

Phil, you traitor.

"Good morning, Ms. Bauer. I hope you were able to enjoy the beautiful weather yesterday. A little vitamin D can do wonders for someone's moods."

Fucking asshole. Familiar heat builds in my fingertips while my eyes remain locked on my computer screen. "You can take your vitamin D and shove it where the sun *doesn't* shine, Wilcox."

Out of the corner of my eye, his steps falter, but his smile only grows wider as he approaches my desk. "I see someone woke up with a case of the Mondays." He chuckles, plopping the bag and cup onto my desk.

Oh, you smug—

Wrapping one hand around the cardboard cup, I remove the plastic lid with the other.

Inside the cup, the brown liquid boils as heat seeps from my flesh. Yanking the poor potted plant to the center of my desk, I dump the hot liquid onto the soil. Without opening the bag, I toss it into the trash can under my desk.

Glaring up at him, I cross my arms over my chest. Cyrus's jaw clenches, but his eyes lower to my tits before slicing back to my face. "What the hell, princess?"

Popping to a stand, I slam my hands down on my desk. The glass splinters under the force. Great, there goes another desk. "I don't know what your motives are, but we're *not* friends. Hell, we're barely even coworkers."

His blue eyes blaze, and I'm not sure if it's with anger or lust.

But the fire in his gaze sends a riot of goosebumps across my skin until I can no longer contain the shiver that rushes down my spine. I cannot give in to this magnetism between us. He's the enemy... *remember?*

"If that's how you want to play it, then that's how we'll play it, *princess*." Shutting down our verbal duel, he turns and stomps to his desk, ignoring me for the rest of the morning.

Once Pen arrives, the day continues with Cyrus giving me the cold shoulder, but I prefer it this way.

For the first time in weeks, I'm able to focus on my work, finishing off the warehouse mockups and leaving a voicemail for Mr. O'Malley regarding his signature on the contract.

It's nearing five o'clock when I come up for air. Grabbing the papers I need, I swing by Penelope's desk on my way to the copy room. "Have a good dinner with your brother. I'll see you tomorrow."

"Night, Annie." She smirks. "Don't kill Cyrus while I'm gone."

My laughter carries down the hallway, and I throw a final goodbye wave over my shoulder.

I'm so engrossed in the whir of the copy machine as it spits out my papers, I don't notice his presence until his spicy scent fills the small room to the brim. "What is your problem with me, princess?"

Spinning away from the copier, I find Cyrus leaning against the doorframe of the copy room, arms crossed over his thick chest, biceps straining against the sleeves of his shirt.

Why does he have to be so fucking attractive?

His eyes trail over me, and I stand an inch taller in my stilettos.

I've been running a little hotter ever since our face-off this morning, so I left my cardigan at my desk, leaving me in a flimsy camisole and my tight pencil skirt.

His tongue peeks out, and I can't peel my eyes away when it runs a path across his lower lip, wetting the plump flesh.

I've managed to avoid him all day, but now he has me trapped in this fucking closet-sized room with his dark vanilla musk creeping into all my pores. "I don't have a problem, Wilcox. Do you?"

With a smirk, my eyes drop to the front of his pants. Sure enough, there's a faint bulge in his dark-gray slacks.

"*You* are my fucking problem, Antoinette." In three giant steps, he has me pinned between his hard chest and the copier. Dipping down, his heated breath fans across the side of my face. "I try to be nice to you. Be a good partner. And you bite my damn head off. Why?"

My throat clicks with a swallow. Ice settles in my veins, freezing my limbs like they're made of stone. Part of me wants to fight back or flee. But the other part wants to stay right here, eating up the heat of his body, relishing the puff of his minty breath along my throat.

Raising my hands, they settle on his pecs, but I don't push him away. "You're in my space and in my head." My voice is a harsh whisper, chest heaving when he skims his nose up the side of my neck. "And I hate it."

At my hissed words, Cyrus pulls back until our mouths are a breath apart. All it would take is a slight tip of my chin and I'd know what his lips feel like. Are they as soft as they look? What does he taste like? Spicy? Maybe a hint of that tempting vanilla?

The clear membrane on my eyes slam shut, breaking me from his penetrating stare. "Just *stop*. Stop bringing me tea every morning. Stop bringing me my favorite bagel. Stop being nice to me." This time, I do push against his chest until he stumbles back, taking his warmth with him. If he was any other man, I'd love to curl against him on a cold night.

But he's not.

He's Cyrus Wilcox.

The man who got me fired once upon a time. Walls back in place, I tighten my jaw, gritting out my next words. "Let's just get through this presentation and hope Andrews lets us go our separate ways afterward."

With shaking hands, I snatch the still warm papers from the copier. I shoulder past him, not stopping until I have my tote bag in hand and make my escape to the roof. An evening flight to the Statue of Liberty should calm my nerves.

I almost gave in to his perfect lips. That was too close for comfort.

CHAPTER 12

Cyrus

Somehow, after our encounter in the copy room, I made it through another day without Antoinette frying me to a crisp. We're in the final push for the O'Malley project, but the tension between us crackles in the air every time we get close.

All I know is my cock's never been harder than when she comes at me with her fiery words and scathing glares. A smarter man might cower and retreat. Too bad I've never been that smart.

I want her.

But I shouldn't.

And she clearly despises how much she wants me. She almost gave in last night. I could *feel* it in the heaving rise and fall of her chest. The blown vertical pupils that are usually mere slits. And, of course, the peaked nipples that stood erect, visible through her thin top like two spotlights in the darkest night.

"One order of chicken chow mein, and one order of beef and broccoli. As requested." Pen slides the white cardboard containers across the conference table. Saliva pools in my mouth as the savory aroma of dinner fills my nose and banishes all thoughts of last night. "Do you need anything else?"

Too busy grabbing the container and ripping the lid open, I don't answer Pen. I'm sure the rumbling of my stomach is audible as I load my chopsticks and shovel the first bite into my mouth.

Antoinette shakes her head, her movements stiff and almost robotic. "Thank you, Pen. Why don't you head home and get some rest? We'll be here for a while yet." Her glare slices to me, the nictitating membrane obscuring her luminous irises briefly before they swing back to Pen. A warm smile replaces her scowl. "I'll see you in the morning."

Pen's cornflower eyes meet mine, delicate eyebrows winging up in question; like she's concerned I can't handle an evening alone with the dragon next to me.

"We'll be fine, Pen," I reassure, chomping on a bite of chicken. "Thank you for your help today. You're truly irreplaceable."

A soft blush paints her cheeks at my compliment.

Over the past few weeks, Pen and I have become an unlikely pair of friends. And I've come to realize how essential a role she plays in keeping Antoinette calm and collected during times of high stress.

I have a feeling there would be a lot more accidental fires around the office without her presence.

"Okay, have a good night. Try not to kill each other." With a wave over her shoulder, she disappears from view, leaving me alone with the woman who despises me.

Focusing my attention back on Antoinette, I notice the small smile tilting one corner of her lush red lips. Twinkling golden eyes linger on the office door as she sighs. She really is beautiful when she's not plotting my demise or verbally berating me. Shaking my head, I banish those thoughts. "Alright, princess. Let's break for dinner, then we can get a fresh start once I'm no longer too hungry to think straight."

"Fine." She huffs and drags the container of beef and broccoli closer to her. Like a gentleman, I grab a pair of chopsticks and toss them to her, followed by a fortune cookie.

Bringing another bite to my lips, the spicy aroma tickles my nose. "Man, that's good. When was the last time you had Chinese food?"

Her lips wrap around the end of the chopsticks as she licks off some of the sauce. When the tips of her little pink forked tongue peek out, I'm convinced she's torturing me on purpose.

Have I imagined what those forks would be like running up and down my hard shaft?

Yes, on several occasions.

I've only been with human women, so there's an added allure to Antoinette. There's a wild beast lingering under her olive skin and part of me wants to get burned by her fiery breath or scratched by her razor-sharp claws.

"It's been a while. I have a personal chef who prepares all my meals, so I prefer to eat at home." Her curt tone puts an end to my runaway thoughts.

Tensions between us have come to an all-time high with all the extra hours we've been working, forced to spend day in and day out together in this suddenly too-small office.

"Sounds boring." I shove another bite of chicken and noodles into my mouth.

Those damn golden eyes roll, making my hand itch with the need to teach her a lesson in manners. But I refrain, gripping my chopsticks until they nearly snap in half.

"Can we please focus on the task at hand," she chides, like I'm a petulant child. "I don't want to be here all night."

"Sure, princess." Setting my food to the side, I roll my chair closer to hers. We're set up at the conference table in the corner of our office, surrounded by windows on two sides, the stars twinkling in the night sky outside.

Exhaustion seeps into me as I give up the fight. It's been a long day, and I want nothing more than to crawl into my bed and sleep, but here I am.

I've gotten as comfortable as I can in my business attire, removing my suit jacket and tie, rolling up my sleeves and unbuttoning the top few buttons on my shirt.

Antoinette has removed her cardigan and heels, left only in a sleeveless retro black-and-white polka dot dress. Combined with her shiny black hair styled with glamorous waves, she's the epitome of a pin-up girl.

At least I have something pretty to gawk at while we work.

My cock agrees, straining against the zipper of my pants, much to my dismay.

"Care to share your plans with the class? Since my deal on the riverfront property fell through, your warehouse is our only chance of impressing the board... and keeping our jobs."

Munching on a piece of broccoli, she shakes her head. The delicate muscles of her throat ripple when she swallows. "That's where you're wrong, Cyrus. This is *my* project. *My* chance to impress the board. Don't try to steal my credit again."

Her accusation takes me back, reeling for a second, before I push it aside. *Choose your battles, Cy.* And this isn't worth the fight. "Whatever you say, princess." I point my chopsticks at the rolls of blueprints on the table. "Show me what you've got."

Grabbing one of the rolls, she unfurls the papers on the tabletop in front of us, and my eyebrows climb further up my forehead with each detail I take in. It's the warehouse, but... *better*. A mix of modern and industrial finishes for what look like condos and commercial spaces. "Where did you get these?"

"I have my connections," she purrs, smoothing a hand over the paper almost lovingly. "My contractor drew up the plans in exchange for giving him the remodel job. He does amazing work, so it was a no-brainer."

I grunt. Fuck, these plans are good. Better than anything I'd come up with. "Explain it to me," I say, tapping a finger on the residential portion of the plans.

"This area," she starts, and my eyes follow her finger. "The top portion of the warehouse would be turned into four luxury condos. Think sleek and industrial. Open ceilings, exposed beams, and pipes. Concrete flooring, mixed with darker woods. Add in modern fixtures and sharp lines. And we should be able to attract a higher end clientele."

Tapping a finger on my chin, my eyes scan over every detail. It's impressive. "Okay, this could work. But what about the bottom of the warehouse?"

Rolling up the first blueprint, she extracts a second from the pile and sets it in place, smoothing the thick paper against the wood of the table. "The lower level would be converted into commercial space featuring a similar modern industrial vibe. The hope is to bridge the gap between city life and suburban life." She holds her hands up like two sides of a scale, evenly weighted. "This could be a game changer for Big York. Break out of the commercial game and dip their toes into residential real estate. Plus, expanding outside the heart of the city would mean more opportunities for new clients and new properties. It's a win-win situation."

Her enthusiasm is hypnotizing. Eyes sparkling while her fingers dance across the papers. Body practically vibrating when she continues to explain the different portions of the blueprint; her voice is bubbly and addicting. I hang on to every word because I've never seen so much emotion from this woman before—well, besides anger.

Joy looks good on her, I decide.

But I can't give in too easily. She does claim to hate me, after all. So I'm silent for a moment, eyes taking in every detail of her plans, from the outdoor bistro seating for a restaurant to the large balconies on the condos that overlook the river. It's the perfect combination of classy and sleek to draw city dwellers out of the city.

It's fucking brilliant.

"You hate it, don't you?" Perfectly arched black eyebrows scrunch together as she gnaws on her bottom lip.

I chuckle, the sound deep and rich as I cross my arms over my chest. Leaning back in my chair, I spin to face her. "On the contrary, princess. This is the perfect idea to get the board's attention. You've really outdone yourself." The clap of my hands echoes around the quiet office in a slow applause. I smirk. "Good job, Bauer."

Her full lips tug at the corners, like she's fighting the reaction, until they finally split into a smile.

A smile that knocks the wind from my lungs as her glittering white teeth are put on display. The cutest fanged canines dig into her bottom lip, pinching the flesh.

Fuck, she's stunning. Glowing from within, her eyes light up like fireworks. Cherry red flushes across her cheeks when her smile somehow grows broader.

Of course, she ruins the moment by opening her damn mouth. "Did you just... compliment me?" Tauntingly, one eyebrow arches in question.

With a low growl in my throat, I scrub a hand over my face, but she continues.

"And your head didn't explode?" As if the sarcasm dripping from her raspy voice wasn't enough, she pushes my buttons further, covering her mouth in a faux gasp.

Clenching my jaw, my teeth clack together when I stand.

She mirrors my movement, standing from her chair and closing the distance between us until my heaving chest brushes her soft breasts.

"Don't push it, princess. Say 'thank you' and move on," I rumble, flipping us and crowding her against the table. It's all too reminiscent of the other night when I cornered her against the copy machine.

That night, I wanted to ruck up her tight dress and make her screams fill the tiny room, but she pushed me away again and ran away with her tail between her legs... metaphorically speaking, of course.

Her ass hits the edge of the table when she leans back, luminous eyes meeting mine, flaring with indignation. "Thank you... *sir*."

Damnit. That title on her ruby lips has my cock springing to life against my will. The thick shaft rubs almost painfully against the placket of my suit pants. "Don't push me, Antoinette."

Raising her chin, she stares down the bridge of her nose at me, lips still curled in a wolfish grin. "Or what, *sir*?"

Based on the gleam in her eyes, she knows exactly what she's doing: pushing me off the cliff into the pit of sexual tension that's been brewing between us for weeks.

I'm only human. I can only resist her for so long before I... snap. And that's exactly what happens. The last measly thread of restraint holding me back frays into a million micro-pieces and I slam my mouth to hers.

CHAPTER 13

Cyrus

F renetic electricity explodes in every nerve ending in my body when our lips seal together. To my surprise, Antoinette doesn't fight me, like she knew this explosion between us was coming before I did.

She's soft and warm, lush curves melting against me when my hands come to rest on the cushion of her hips.

Antoinette returns the kiss tenfold, teeth gnashing against my lower lip and pulling until a grunt tumbles from my throat. Ever the opportunist, she snakes that damn forked tongue into my mouth. And it's *everything* and more than I expected.

The texture is rough, almost like a cat's tongue. As she explores my mouth, a shiver rushes through me and every hair on my body rises to attention. *Her* attention. I want every last drop she'll give me. Each stroke of our tongues fills the hole in my heart.

She curls the thick, forked muscles of her tongue around the width of mine and begins to stroke up and down... like she would with my cock. "Holy shit!" I blurt, pulling back until I'm met by scorching metallic eyes, my hands resting on her slender shoulders. "Your tongue! I knew it was forked, but it's—"

"Prehensile," she purrs, skating the pointed tips of her tongue across her bottom lip until it's coated with a sheen of saliva. "Imagine what else I could do with it."

I shudder, heart practically beating out of my chest. Even the thought of the rough texture against my throbbing shaft has me nearly unloading into my slacks, like a fucking teenaged boy.

Squeezing her shoulders in my grasp, I assess her expression, eyebrows arched in question as she waits. "Antoinette, are you sure you want to do this? I know things are tense between us, but once we cross this line," I say, releasing her shoulder to draw an imaginary line between us, "it'll change everything."

What I don't say is that one time with her won't be enough.

Once I sink into her sweet heat and get a taste of her pleasure, I'll be addicted. Of that, I'm one hundred percent certain.

She may hate me, but I've started to doubt just how much I really hate her. The past week or so, I've been putting on a show because it seemed like what she needed to function in our working relationship.

But I'm not so sure anymore.

Almost like she's patronizing me, she pats my chest with her manicured hand, black nails gleaming in the dim fluorescent light. "It doesn't have to change anything, Cyrus. This is merely... a release. A purging of bad energy, if you will."

I nod, but I'm not sure I agree with her.

"Now, fuck me like you hate me." Her voice is demanding and harsh, chin tilted up.

Domineering and commanding.

She thinks she's the one in charge. Not today, Antoinette. "Oh, but princess, I do hate you," I retort, goading her.

"Good, then it shouldn't be a problem." Delicate fingers grip the sides of my shirt and tug until the buttons give way and ping somewhere to the ground. But I don't have an ounce of care in my body as I clamp my hands around her wide, plush hips and hoist her onto the table.

Long forgotten are the blueprints and our dinner.

"You're fucking infuriating, princess," I growl, my lips trailing down her neck to the swell of her breasts, where they peek out of her dress. "So feisty and hard-headed. But so damn sexy."

My hands shove at the hem of her dress, pushing the soft fabric up her thighs and hips until it bunches around her waist.

A flash of vibrant fuchsia catches my eyes when I dip my head. The vivid lace covering her mound is drenched, a wet spot prominent on the front of the pinkish-purple material. "Are you dripping for *me*, princess? Your self-proclaimed rival?"

Throwing her head back, she groans, long and low, as my fingers press into the sopping lace and strum her clit. Hips rocking ever-so-subtly, she whines, "Yes, sir."

Sir. This time, the word has a feral possessiveness flaring through me, and my hands shake when I grip the sides of her panties and tear them from her body.

I nearly swallow my own tongue at the first glimpse of her cunt. Arousal wets her plump flesh, and I catch sight of her throbbing clit when she tips her hips and spreads her legs unabashedly. The need to touch her wins out, and I run my thumb through her slit until it's coated in *her*. "What am I going to do with you, Antoinette? You fucking hate me, but this—"

Squelching fills the air as my fingers pump in and out of her channel. She's soaked. The warmth on my fingers has the anticipation of shoving my cock into her growing in my body. "This sopping cunt says otherwise, princess. It says you want me. You need me. You can't fucking resist me." I continue, lips carving into a smug grin while I hover over her mouth.

"You're so arrogant, Wilcox. Just fuck me before I change my mind."

I doubt she would. And as much as I'm enjoying our little power struggle, I do want to fuck her. Pre-cum drips down my shaft from how much I want to fuck her.

The generous curves she puts on display in her fitted dresses and skirts. The scarlet red lipstick she paints on her lips every day. The sleek retro curls of her shiny black hair. All these things combined make her my dream woman.

Even her feisty attitude adds to the allure. She's not afraid to be herself and go after what she wants.

Right now, apparently that's me.

Not waiting for my response, her skilled hands work my belt buckle open, followed by the button and fly of my pants. With a forceful shove, she has my pants and boxers falling from around my hips and pooling at my ankles, caught by my brown leather loafers.

Her throaty groan surrounds us as she wraps her hand around my shaft and strokes. My knees buckle, and I have to catch myself with my hands on the edge of the table.

"You're bigger than I expected. I thought for sure you were compensating for something with your insufferable personality."

Surrounding her hand with mine, I force her fingers tighter around my aching length and glide our hands up and down my cock. My hips buck softly, chasing pleasure as I moan. "Joke's on you, princess. I'm not compensating for anything."

"You're so irritating," she groans, head falling back as she rubs the leaking head of my cock against her swollen clit. "Just shut up and make me come already. Otherwise, I'll do it myself."

Not on my watch. Knocking her hand to the side, I line myself up with her opening and shove inside. "Oh, fuck." The whispered words fall from my lips when the head of my cock slips inside her warm opening. "You're wet and tight. I knew you'd be fucking perfect."

Her strong thighs squeeze around my hips while her feet press against my ass, welcoming me into her sweet body with an urgency flowing between us.

Bottoming out, I give her a second to adjust to my girth. Did her earlier compliment have me preening internally? Abso-fucking-lutely.

Once her muscles relax around my shaft, I ease out of her heat. But as I'm shoving back inside, I'm met by a ribbed texture that has my breath catching. Wide-eyed, I weave my fingers into the back of her hair and tug her head up until I meet her glowing eyes.

"Are you ribbed?" The question is choked and hoarse. Each drive of my hips has my body overcome with pleasure, the beginnings of my orgasm taking root at the base of my spine.

"Female dragons have lots of unique sexual qualities," she purrs, hands braced on the table behind her while her hips rock, taking my cock deeper into her slick channel.

I think I've finally died and gone to heaven. Every drag of her ribbed pussy walls on my shaft has me ready to blow my damn load.

But I can't let her think I'm some selfish chump who doesn't know how to get a woman off. No, that won't do, so I dig my fingers into the fat of her hips and pick up my pace, pounding into her while I fixate on the expression of ecstasy on her face.

Mouth split open on a chorus of moans; her eyes are liquid with lust. Her walls tighten around me.

Yes, she's almost there!

Except, her hands come up and shove against my chest. My cock is dislodged from her warmth, feet caught in my pants around my ankles as I topple into the office chair behind me.

"For one." Her silken voice coats my sweat-slicked skin when she stands from the table. I can't pull my eyes away from her hand as it reaches behind her and lowers the zipper of her dress. "Female dragons like to be in charge during sex." The black-and-white fabric falls to the ground, revealing a matching fuchsia bra.

Vibrant lace hugs her tits, pushing them together to create a valley I want to run my tongue through.

Under my intense stare, her nipples pucker against the thin lace until they're on full display.

I let my eyes travel the length of her body. Her curves are luscious and thick. An ample chest gives way to a narrow waist, only to flare into wide hips.

Bringing my fist to my mouth, I bite my knuckle to stifle a groan. I bet if I was behind her, her ass would jiggle with every step.

Dark curls draw my eyes to her glistening cunt. Damn, I need my dick back inside her before I explode.

"Holy shit." As she glides closer, I follow the subtle bounce of her olive-toned breasts. Finally coming to stand between my spread thighs, my hands automatically latch onto the excess flesh rounding her hips. My poor, ignored cock jumps against my abs, eager to be hugged in her perfect heat. "You're stunning."

She chuckles, but doesn't remove my hands. "Now, be a good boy," she coos, fingers stroking through my hair as she straddles my lap. "And make me come."

I nearly swallow my tongue when the ridges of her pussy engulf my cock again. She slams herself down until her pillowy ass meets my tensed quad muscles.

Finding purchase on her hips, I'm held captive beneath her lush body as she finds her rhythm, rocketing both our bodies toward their peaks.

The soft swell of her breasts bounces in my face, and I want nothing more than to rip the lacy cups down and expose her flesh.

So I do.

Letting go of her hips, I peel the cups down, setting her glorious tits free. Beaded nipples tempt my tongue while she continues to bounce on my cock, moaning like a banshee.

"Damn, princess, you sure know how to ride a cock," I murmur as I chase one dark-pink nipple with my mouth, trying my damndest to get my lips around it.

Without faltering, she slams a hand over my mouth, tilting my head back in the process. "Shut up, Wilcox. You're ruining it."

I gulp at the sheer unhinged need beaming from her molten eyes.

Her sharp *claws* dig into my cheeks, quieting me. But her hips never stop.

The dragon in her breaks free, tendrils of smoke wafting from each nostril and iridescent black scales climbing up her forearms.

Her face is the picture of a woman possessed, one on a mission. More shimmering scales rip through the skin of her high cheekbones. Hypnotic golden eyes glowing brighter than the sun. "When I remove my hand, the only words I want to hear from these pretty lips are 'yes, ma'am.' Do you understand?"

I nod. She looks every inch the predator that lurks under her flesh. And, for some reason, my cock is harder than it's ever been.

She removes her hand. "Say. Them."

Meeting her fiery gaze with my icy stare, I grit out, "Yes, ma'am."

Those words have her pussy clenching around me until I groan. A wicked smile paints her face. "Good boy. Now, put your mouth where it belongs." She shoves my face between her breasts, and I'm all too happy to lick and suck at the scorching flesh. It's so hot, I'm surprised I don't get burned. Her dragon must be right there, ready to break free.

One hard suck of her nipple has her cunt locking around me as she comes. Clamped in her vise grip, I can't hold back any longer. Pleasure sling-shots down my spine and into my balls until I'm unloading every drop of cum into her tight pussy.

"Holy shit," I groan, nuzzling her chest.

Her fingers are still threaded through my hair, holding me to her heaving bosom. The tight muscles of her cunt haven't loosened at all since our combined orgasms. Tugging on her hips, I try to lift her off my lap, but I'm... stuck.

"Princess, ummm. We seem to have a problem. My cock is stuck in you."

The harsh laugh from her throat has me smiling. Maybe this is the start of something between us. I can do that—work side by side during the day and fuck like animals after business hours.

"You're *locked* inside me, Wilcox. It's a breeding thing. But don't worry. A human man can't get a female dragon pregnant, anyway. Just give it a moment."

The disdain in her words has my stomach sinking. Was this a one-and-done thing for her? Am I merely a novelty?

"Antoinette," I grunt. Pulling away from her chest, I run a hand up the side of her neck in an attempt to guide her face toward me. But she won't budge, gaze fixed on the starry night outside the windows.

Once her cunt releases me, she doesn't waste a second to extricate herself from my arms. Standing before me, she adjusts her bra to cover her amazing breasts, and my stomach drops. With a curt tone and snapped words, she says, "This cannot happen again, Mr. Wilcox."

"What?"

Grabbing her clothes and bag, she bolts from the office before my brain can comprehend what's happening.

Finally catching up, I wrangle my pants up and chase after her. "Antoinette, wait!"

A flash of dark hair guides me to the stairs leading to the roof. I sprint up the steps as fast as I can but, fuck, her shifter speed gives her an advantage. Colliding with the roof access door, I stumble through the opening right as Antoinette's body bursts into flames.

In her place stands a black and gold dragon the size of a small car. With an exhale of fire, she roars and flaps her wings, shooting into the midnight sky.

My mouth gapes, eyes fixed on her shrinking form until she disappears into the darkness.

Not only is she radiant in human form, but she's majestic in dragon form, too.

And I'm screwed because that was the best sex I've ever had. Already, the need for more is growing in my veins.

Running a hand through my rumpled hair, I clutch the ends and blow out a breath. "Tomorrow is gonna be interesting." Antoinette ran out of here like she was literally on fire, so I have no idea what I'm in for tomorrow morning.

Will she bite my head off and go back to hating me?

Will she give me the cold shoulder? My breath catches, an invisible fist tightening around my lungs. Somehow, her silence is worse than our verbal sparring.

Or will she see reason and give in to this inferno of lust blazing between us? Something tells me the sex is going to be even better the second time.

The next morning, at six on the dot, I walk into our office to find Antoinette already at her desk, clacking away on her keyboard. I can't help the smile that lights up my face. She's not avoiding me after what we did last night. That has to be a good sign, right?

Coming to stand in front of her desk, I wait for her piercing gaze to meet mine, but she doesn't look away from her computer screen. "Good morning, Mr. Wilcox," she says without giving me a morsel of her attention, fingers still typing on her keyboard.

A fire lights in my veins, but I tamp it down for now. Flying off into a fit of anger won't do any good. And it will certainly send Antoinette into her own rage spiral.

Smile still plastered on my face, I greet her. "Good morning, Ms. Bauer. How was your evening?" Frigid woman. Is she really going to ignore me after last night?

Her golden gaze finally lifts from the computer screen, emotionless and cold. "Fine, thank you. How was your evening, Mr. Wilcox?" Her dainty hands stack one on top of the other as she waits for my response.

Sighing, I lean down and brace my hands on her desk, invading her space. "Antoinette, are we really not going to address what happened?"

Perfectly sculpted black eyebrows climb on her forehead. "Address what? It was a momentary lapse in judgment. I can assure you, it will not happen again."

The fuck? My blood boils and my chest heaves. Is she fucking kidding right now? "Are you—"

Turning back to her computer, she cuts me off. "If you'll excuse me, I have a lot of work to do this morning." Flicking her wrist, she shoos me away like a naughty schoolboy.

Since sharing a space with her, I've learned that once Antoinette Bauer dismisses you, there's no reasoning with her. So I trudge to my desk and sort through her words in my head.

Momentary lapse in judgment.

What the actual fuck?

Am I the only one who felt the fire between us blazing out of control?

How do I get this infuriating woman to dismantle her castle walls and let me in?

CHAPTER 14

Antoinette

I can't be here anymore. Whatever spicy cologne he's wearing is clogging my brain and clouding my judgment. The usual annoyance and even rage that I feel toward Cyrus has turned into something much worse. *Lust.*

It rushes through my veins like a raging river threatening to wash away everything in its path.

If I don't get out of this office—out of his gravitational pull—I'm liable to fuck him again.

And that absolutely cannot happen.

Last night was a mistake. Emotions were high after landing my dream contractor and seeing the first drawings. It was us blowing off steam, nothing more.

Right?

A wave of nausea washes over me and takes hold in my gut. I don't do attachments. I do nameless one-night stands when the sexual itch gets unbearable. Why does this human man make me want to throw everything out the window and fuck him again?

No one, human or monster, has ever had such a pull over me before. All I could think about last night as I tossed and turned in bed was how wet he'd made my stupid cunt with his filthy words.

I'm used to being in control during sex, but last night, a part of me wanted to relinquish control to Cyrus.

No. I can't do that.

If I let him inside my body again, he may end up inside my heart, too.

Would that be so bad?

"Yes," I hiss under my breath, hoping Cyrus doesn't hear.

A bead of sweat drips down the side of my face. I tug at the collar of my shirt. My skin is scorching to the touch, hotter than normal.

My dragon presses to get free, which causes my flesh to tighten and pull.

With shaking hands, I power down my laptop. I undock it and shove it into my black leather tote bag.

Slinging the strap over my shoulder, I clear my throat and stand so forcefully that the chair rolls away and bounces off the wall of windows behind my desk. "I'm not feeling well. I'll be working from home for the remainder of the day. Please follow up on the O'Malley contract in my absence." I keep my voice neutral and avoid making eye contact as I rush out.

It's not until I'm two steps from the door that his voice rumbles from behind me.

"Yes, princess."

The nickname gives me pause, and it lights a strange buzz between my legs.

No, no, no! I cannot be attracted to Cyrus Wilcox.

He's the enemy.

The sales thief.

Nodding, I scurry by Penelope's empty desk. It's only a little after six in the morning, so she isn't here yet.

Making my way to the rooftop, I pull my phone from my bag. If I've learned anything from Pen, it's that only one thing will fix this situation: wine and donuts.

> **Me: Meet at my place ASAP. We're playing hooky.**

> **Pen: Uh-oh. What did Wilcox do?**

> **Me: Bring donuts and I'll explain.**

> **Pen: That bad? Be there soon.**

In the meantime, there's one other option to burn off the electric energy surging through my veins.

Hopping on one foot, I slip one heel off, then the other. Shoving them into my bag, I sprint the rest of the way to the roof access door.

My clammy palms stick to the fabric when I tug the remainder of my clothes from my body and hastily stuff them into the bag to join my shoes.

I barely have time to drop my tote bag to the ground before my body bursts into flames and my dragon springs free. My roar ripples through the crisp morning air as I loop a claw through the strap of my bag and rocket into the sky.

All the while, I can't help but wonder... *What if last night wasn't a mistake?*

"Have no fear, backup has arrived!" Penelope's sing-song voice soothes my frazzled nerves. Closing the penthouse door behind her, she whirls to face me with her arms wrapped around a pink cardboard box. Donuts from Cream Me Up.

Since flying in the balcony door of my apartment, I've been pacing a line in the floor—a difficult task, considering it's tile.

I'm not even sure when I changed into my favorite silk pajama set or washed off my makeup.

"Oh shit. You're pacing... and muttering... and..." Her voice cuts off on a cough, and she fans a hand in front of her face. Plumes of smoke fill the air around me, swirling their way over to the door.

Shit. It's a wonder I didn't set off the smoke alarms. Wouldn't be the first time. And probably won't be the last.

"Annie, you're spiraling." She shrugs off her trench coat, lays it on the entryway table, and extends a hand to me. "Come here."

Crossing the room, I slip my hand into hers. The nausea in my stomach dissipates a little when her warm fingers tighten around mine. Pen tugs me to the couch and all but shoves me onto it before draping a blanket over my shoulders.

I don't need it; my skin is still hot to the touch.

But I've learned over the years this is how Pen comforts people. So I hug the blanket closer, wrapping it over my fists and tucking them under my chin, while she grabs wineglasses and plates from the kitchen.

"Okay," she demands. She places a nearly overflowing wineglass in my hand. Then Pen sets a plate full of donuts on the coffee table in front of me. Stuffing half a donut into her mouth, she plops into her favorite corner of the couch and says, "Spill. What the hell happened after I left last night?" Her words are jumbled around a mouthful of fried dough. If I wasn't so overwhelmed, I'd be laughing.

Expelling all the air from my lungs, I suck in a breath and rush the words out, eyes locked on the coffee table in front of me. "IsleptwithCyrusWilcox."

Grabbing a donut, I shove half of it into my mouth and focus on the sugary goodness as it coats my tongue.

When I finally muster the courage to turn toward Pen, her mouth is gaping like a fish out of water, and her eyes are as big as saucers. Once she's regained her composure, she clears her throat and says, "I must have misheard you. Did you say you slept with Cyrus? Cyrus Wilcox? As in the man you can barely stand to be in the same room as, let alone have a civilized conversation with?"

I nod.

Her expression morphs into one of childlike joy as she bounces on the couch and claps her hands. "I have so many questions. How? Where? What was it like? Tell me *everything*!"

"Pen, you're missing the point completely. This is *not* something to be celebrating! It was a mistake. Clearly, I had a lapse in judgment and let the stress of this project get the better of me. Okay?"

One blonde eyebrow arches up on her forehead, and I know she doesn't believe a word out of my mouth. Honestly, I'm starting to doubt them myself. "Who are you trying to convince, Annie? Because if you ask me, you and Cyrus are the perfect match. You're both hardworking and motivated. And as much as you don't want to admit it... he is intelligent and competent at his job."

I scoff, shoving the other half of the donut into my mouth and crossing my arms.

"Imagine what you could do if you cooperated and worked together."

"I don't need anyone else—besides you. I've made it almost 200 years on my own. Why should things be different now?" But as the words tumble from my lips, familiar doubt creeps in. I can't ignore the pit of loneliness in my soul anymore, as if part of me is missing.

A warm set of arms wrap around me, and I sink into Pen's embrace. She's like the little sister I never had. Dragons only produce one offspring in their lifetime, so I grew up utterly alone.

Pulling back, she cups my face. "Annie, would it be so bad if you let him in?"

Moisture wells in my eyes, and I hate it. I'm not a crier. Crying doesn't solve problems, so it's useless. "I-I don't know anymore, Pen. I'm so confused. I've never reacted to another being—let alone a human man—like this before. He makes me so irrationally angry, but he also pushes me and challenges me. He makes me strive to be better."

Releasing me, she sits back and smirks, which causes the adorable dimple in her cheek to appear. "And the sex? How was it?"

I roll my eyes so hard I'm afraid they'll get stuck in the back of my head. Shit stirrer.

I should lie and tell her it was abysmal, so that I have another reason to stay away from Cyrus. But Pen is my best friend, and the truth slips out easily. "It was fucking amazing. Would you expect anything less from the man?" One side of my mouth hitches into a smirk.

"I knew it!" she crows, both dimples on her cheeks popping this time when her face lights up with a smile. I can't even be mad that she's goading me. Pen is like a perpetual ray of sunshine on my darkest day. She's my lighthouse in the raging storm when my dragon's temper gets the better of me.

I don't know what I'd do without her.

"Okay," I say while she continues to smirk at me over the lip of her wineglass. "Enough gloating. What should I do?"

"You *talk* to him, Annie. He was a willing participant in last night's events, yes?"

Heat sears my cheeks when I think back to the way I rode Cyrus like my own personal stallion in his office chair. Gulping down some wine, I swallow and squeak, "Yes."

Penelope's fingers fly across her phone screen. Wait. No. That's not her phone case. It's *mine*!

"What are you doing with my phone?" I shoot a hand out, attempting to grab it from her.

Completely ignoring my question, she holds the phone out of my reach. Blue eyes peering up at me, another smug grin pops onto her innocent face. "Then he must find you attractive. Now, you clear the air and decide if you want more, or if you want to go back to hating him."

Locking my phone, she plops it in my lap and grabs another donut. "And you've got about fifteen minutes to figure it out because Cyrus is on his way here."

Meddling little shit. My jaw hits the floor. I flounder to grab my phone. Pulling up my messages, sure enough, there's a text chain with Cyrus, requesting his emergency assistance at my apartment. "Penelope!"

She cackles, finishing the last of her wine and standing up from the couch. "Sometimes you just need to get out of your own way, Annie. You and Cyrus could be something truly amazing together. Have you seen the way he watches you at the office?" She fans herself, cheeks pink from the alcohol and her horny thoughts. "I'd give my life savings for someone to be that infatuated with me. And don't worry, I'll stick around to make sure you don't kill him."

"You're lucky I love you so much." In my heart, I know Cyrus and I can't continue at this rate. We're headed down a path that will make us bitter and jaded, scarred by hatred. If the alternative is letting my guard down? I don't know if I'm even capable of that.

Either way, I have—I glance at the time on my phone—about ten minutes to decide.

CHAPTER 15

Cyrus

Heat seeps through the to-go cup and into my hand, the faint aroma of lavender filling my nose where I stand outside Antoinette's apartment door.

When her texts hit my phone, I almost couldn't believe my eyes. I'd just sent a follow-up email to Mr. O'Malley, regarding why he hadn't signed our contracts, when my phone chimed on my desk. Antoinette Bauer requesting my assistance at her apartment.

Color me intrigued.

The way she stormed out of the office earlier had me thinking she'd be radio silent for the rest of the day. Yet, by midmorning, my phone was buzzing across my desk as text after text came through.

On the way to her apartment, I stopped at her favorite diner. A sort of peace offering in case I'm walking into an all-out war.

Lavender chamomile should settle the dragon hiding under her chilly exterior.

Knock. Knock.

My knuckles rap against the metal door, and I lean against the frame, waiting for a response.

As I'm raising my hand to knock again, the door swings inward, revealing... "Penelope?"

Lips curled in a mischievous smile, she waves. "Hi, Cyrus. Won't you come in?" With a sweep of her hand, she beckons me inside.

My eyebrows are stuck at my hairline as I follow Pen into the apartment. At first glance, it's sleek and minimal. The modern lines and neutral color palette are fitting for Antoinette. But I notice there aren't any personal touches.

No photos on the walls.

No random seashells found on the beach.

No heirloom knickknacks you want to get rid of, but can't because your mother gave them to you.

Upon further inspection, the open floor plan is cold and lifeless, not what I'd expect from the fiery woman sitting on the couch.

"What's the emergency?" I rumble, approaching Antoinette. Her usual corporate armor is noticeably absent, face free of makeup and curvy body shrouded by a cream knit blanket. The sight of her in the comfort of her home has my heart racing.

Damn, she's beautiful.

Without makeup, she appears younger. Dark lashes frame her glowing metallic eyes when they raise to meet mine. A glimpse of shimmering black scales peek out on her cheekbones.

"That would be my doing." Penelope's voice has my gaze pulling from Antoinette to the bubbly blonde as she sits on the couch, crossing one knee over the other and stacking her hands on top.

My head swings toward Antoinette again, eyes widening, waiting for an explanation.

Antoinette's body deflates with a sigh, the blanket slipping from her shoulder to reveal the thin navy-blue strap of her top—and the flawless olive skin I've been dreaming about sinking my teeth into.

Even more so after last night.

"Pen messaged you from my phone, but, now that you're here"—she shrugs—"we should probably clear the air after what happened last night."

My throat clicks with a swallow, and my hand, suddenly clammy, slips around the flimsy cup in my grasp. Bending down, I set it on the coffee table before I accidentally drop it and spill tea all over Antoinette's stark-white rug.

She was so standoffish this morning; I thought for sure we would go right back to tip-toeing around each other at the office, desperately trying to avoid any more feuds. But hope trickles into my body, filling me like the droplets of a summer rain.

Please tell me she wants to do it again, or—wishful thinking—try for more.

Her voice, softer and more timid than normal, interrupts my spiraling thoughts. "I-Is that for me?"

I peel my eyes away from the to-go cup in question and find myself engrossed in the twinkle of stars in her eyes. "Yeah, princess. Lavender chamomile. Is there somewhere private we can talk?" I match her tone, keeping my voice gentle and soothing.

Slender fingers wrap around the cup, taking it with her when she stands from the couch, blanket still clutched around her body with one hand. Like a dutiful puppy, I follow close behind her.

"In here," she says, leading me down a short hallway and into a large bedroom, shutting the door behind us.

One wall is floor-to-ceiling glass. An oversized sliding door opens onto a balcony. The view is exquisite. Mid-morning rays of sun cascade all around us, creating countless rainbows on the soft purple walls.

"This," I say, spinning to take in more of the room. "This is how I pictured your apartment. Not whatever that is out there." I hook a thumb over my shoulder, in the direction of the living room and kitchen. Cold and boring.

"What do you mean?" She perches on the end of the large floor bed. All different shades of purple surround her, from the deepest eggplant of the sheets, to the palest silvery lilac of the fuzzy blanket she's toying with.

My fingers graze the leaves of a plant where it trails along the top of her dresser, the light wood a stark contrast to the deep green of the leaves. "Out there, everything is so cold and impersonal. But here, this room screams Antoinette. Sophisticated and strong. Rich and full of fight. But still soft and feminine." Strings of fairy lights cascade down the walls, twinkling in the sunlight. I can only imagine how magical it would be at night, drifting to sleep while surrounded by a million stars.

She clears her throat, and I stop my perusal of her space. This is clearly her safe place, so her letting me in here is telling on a whole other level.

"This is my nest," she states.

There's a deep plum, velvet wing-back chair near the balcony door. I take a seat and give her my full attention. "Like a bird?"

Her golden eyes roll, but she chuckles. Soft and husky. It warms my chest. I want more of that sound. "No. Like a *dragon*." As her hand waves through the air, I notice the scales now climb up the backs of her hands. Her fingers are tipped with dainty black claws.

What would it be like to have the biting sting of those claws against my skin while I'm deep inside her?

My cock thickens in my pants, but now isn't the time. We need to clear the air and figure out what the hell is going on between us.

Turning toward me, her second eyelids blink rapidly before remaining open. "Dragons are collectors. Some may call us hoarders. Whatever you want to call it, we seek comfort in our belongings."

I scoot the chair an inch closer to the bed and rest my elbows on my knees. "You mean like in fairy tales? The dragon always protects its treasure."

She shrugs, picking at the label of the to-go cup. "Not quite. The fairy tales aren't totally accurate. We hoard what we crave. So if a dragon desires riches, they'll gather valuable things. That's where the myth comes from."

My eyes flit around the room once more. I don't see anything shiny or outright valuable. It's mostly pillows and blankets. Lush green plants fill up every corner of the room and hang from decorative hooks along the massive windows. The sheer curtains in the doorway billow in the breeze. "Okay, what do you collect, Ms. Bauer?"

Her gaze stays locked on the cup in her hands, shoulders rounded. This is such a different side of her. One I've never seen before. Meek and mild—almost scared.

Vulnerable.

But I crave to experience every side of Antoinette... if she'll let me.

Even as silence fills the airy space, I don't press her to speak. Something tells me she needs time to work up the courage and peel back the curtain.

Finally, she tilts her head up and her eyes drip with sadness, the normal molten gold now cooler and dimmed.

I don't like it.

Fisting my hands on my thighs, I resist the urge to cross the room and pull her into a hug.

"This is hard for me, Cyrus. I'm not used to anyone being in my space."

Her admission warms something deep inside of me, like she's willing to let me in after what happened between us last night. Maybe it wasn't just a heat of the moment kind of thing for her, like I'd initially assumed.

"I hoard things I find comforting because, for as long as I can remember, I've craved companionship. This type of hoarding isn't normal for dragons."

"Why?" My eyebrows crouch low over my eyes. "What do you mean?"

Shaking her head, she huffs a laugh and stands from the bed. The blanket falls away to reveal her luscious curves. A navy-blue silk tank top and matching silk pants encase her sinful body.

Damn, she even looks sexy in pajamas.

"I shouldn't even be telling you any of this. I don't know you. And I certainly don't like you. But Pen got in my head, and I thought I could do this." She waves her arm toward me, the usual flames simmering behind her eyes again.

"Do what? I'm a little lost here, princess. Care to share with the class?" I'm standing now, too. Chest heaving as her anger radiates toward me.

Black claw raised in the air, she points an accusing finger at me. "You hurt me once before. Who's to say you, won't do it again? No. I won't let you in. Pen is wrong."

Her words don't make sense to me, like my brain is scrambling them before I can comprehend. "What are you talking about?"

"Ten years ago, you took my job. And, maybe, you're planning to do the same thing now? I worked my ass off to get that client to take me seriously, and I was this close—" She holds her thumb and forefinger up in a pinched gesture. "This fucking close to landing the sale. You—You waltzed in the next day and stole it right out from under my feet. You screwed me over, Cyrus. I got fired for losing that sale." Her voice softens as she trails off, eyes glued to my chest.

My stomach drops. "Antoinette, I didn't even know you were gunning for that sale. One of my buddies told me about a property up for sale, and I took advantage of the tip. Plus, I was a fucking dumbass back then." The joke doesn't land, and my laughter falls dead when her mouth twitches downward. "Look at me please, princess." Stepping in front of her, I brace my finger under her chin and tip her face up until I'm met by beautiful, luminous eyes. "If I'd known you were working the same job, I would have backed off. I promise it wasn't anything malicious on my end."

Wide eyes search my face. Her mouth opens, like she wants to say something, but she closes it, silence stretching between us.

"I'm sorry, Antoinette. I was a cocky asshole, but life took something precious from me after that, and I'm trying to be a better person. I'm sorry I hurt you, and I'm sorry if that's the cause of all this animosity between us. But the truth is, I'm tired of fighting. Aren't you?"

Ever-so-subtly, she nods, and I slip my hand down to the side of her throat. Under the skin, her heart thrums like hummingbird wings. "Y-yeah, I'm tired of hating you, too."

A soft smile creeps onto my face. "Okay, then, where do we go from here? Because there's clearly chemistry between us."

Her cheeks darken, as if she's remembering our little scandalous "overtime" from last night.

Thumb stroking her pulse point, I continue. "I like you, princess. And I'd like to know more about you." I back up a step, head swiveling around the room. "For starters, what does Antoinette Bauer do when she plays hooky?"

Her lips split into a lopsided smile. There she is.

Sauntering to the door, her shoulders are pulled back as she swings the door wide and calls out, "Pen! We're gonna need pizza and beer. We're all playing hooky!"

A cheer comes from the other room. "On it!"

CHAPTER 16

Cyrus

"And the final rose goes to... Felicia." On screen, the woman bursts into tears when a minotaur dressed in a tux, that's clearly been custom made for his massive frame, hands her a red rose. She clutches the flower to her chest. The sequins on her purple evening gown shimmer under what I can only assume are production lights.

Rolling my eyes, I snag another piece of greasy pizza from the cardboard box on the coffee table, the TV show droning on in the background. "I can't believe you watch this trash. It's all fake. And what kind of man could date multiple women at the same time... right in front of each other."

A scoff from my right has my head turning in Antoinette and Penelope's direction. Both women's eyes were glued to the TV screen a second ago, but now they're laser-focused on me.

"It's not about the quality of the show, Cyrus," Antoinette explains, pulling the blanket tighter around her shoulders. I still can't get over how relaxed she's been around me all day. Honestly, I'm a little surprised. "It's supposed to be a mindless escape after a long, stressful day."

"No thinking required," Penelope chimes in before shoving the last bite of pepperoni pizza into her mouth. "I should probably go, though. It's getting late, and I have to be up early tomorrow. One of my bosses is a real hard-ass." She winks and knocks shoulders with Antoinette.

Both women stand from the couch and head to the front door. I hang back, standing by the couch to observe their relationship. Penelope slips on her jacket before pulling Antoinette in for a hug.

At a glance, they act more like sisters or friends, not boss and subordinate.

After my conversation with Antoinette earlier, I get the sense she leads a solitary, maybe even lonely, life. Knowing she has someone kind and good, like Penelope, looking after her, warms something deep inside me.

I've come to terms with the fact I have feelings for Antoinette. I don't know how deep they run... yet. If this is surface level, scratching an itch. Or something bone-deep, like soulmates. But I want to take the leap and find out—hopefully she does, too.

Sidling up to the door, I stuff my hands in my pants pockets. "Goodnight, Penelope."

She waves before disappearing down the hallway.

Clearing my throat, I shove the ball of nerves in my gut down as far as it will go. Fuck, why do I feel like a high school punk leaning in for his first kiss?

Antoinette is the first woman, well, ever to make me nervous. She's confident and commanding... maybe even a little scary. But I *want* to be around her.

Dipping down, I cup her cheek and press a kiss against the warm flesh. The black scales peeking through are rough against my lips. When I pull back, her jaw falls slack on a sigh. "I'm gonna head out, too. I'll see you in the morning."

Golden eyes burn into me as she peers up from beneath a curtain of thick, dark lashes. "Stay." The word is so soft, I almost miss it.

"What?" My hand falls to my side.

Antoinette reaches out, weaving her fingers through mine. Eyebrows raised, my gaze locks onto where she grips my fingers. Her hand is so small compared to mine.

Slowly, my eyes trail over her pajamas. Even in leisure clothes, she's classy. The silky fabric hugs her figure like it was tailor made specifically for her. My perusal slows on her throat, where the delicate muscles tighten with an audible swallow. She runs her other hand down the silky material of her pajama bottoms. Is she nervous?

"This—" She clears her throat, dropping my hand and crossing her arms around her middle, like a shield. "It isn't easy for me to ask for help. I've been on my own so long that I'm not used to needing anyone else."

Her words send my stomach swooping. Warmth spreads through me at the idea that maybe I've clawed my way behind her icy walls.

But I tread lightly, stepping into her and hooking my finger under her chin, forcing her molten stare to mine. "And you need *me*?"

Plush lips purse and twist to the side, one delicate shoulder lifting. When it falls again, the thin strap of her sleep tank slips down her shoulder. "It appears so. Although I don't entirely understand it."

Without thinking, I run a finger over her collarbone. So delicate. So beautiful.

My touch glides down over the toned cap of her shoulder to where the strap rests against her upper arm. Slipping it back in place, I ask, "What's not to understand?"

Ignoring my question, she reaches behind me and flips the lock on the door. Then she guides me by the hand down the hall to her bedroom.

Now that the sun has receded below the horizon, the twinkle lights along the ceiling cast the room in a moody glow. It suits her.

Peeling back the covers, she settles in the bed and pats the spot next to her before picking up our earlier conversation. "For one, you drive me absolutely insane. Why would I *need* you?"

A booming chuckle rips from my chest, and I plop back on the bed. She bounces, huffing and crossing her arms when the mattress finally comes to a stop.

Seeing her vulnerability has my earlier nerves settling to a low hum beneath my skin.

"You're looking at the situation all wrong, princess." Not for the first time, I track the shiver that works down her spine at my use of the pet name she once despised... or so she says. "What if the competitive nature between us merely pushes you to be better? What if my being around is a *good* thing?"

"I guess only time will tell. I haven't burned you to a crisp... yet." One black eyebrow arches as her eyes twinkle at me. I swear the corner of her mouth lifts into a minuscule smile.

"You mean *accidentally*, right?"

This time, a wicked smirk flashes across her lips. Gone almost too quickly for me to notice. "Perhaps." Her face sobers; a gusted sigh pushes from her mouth before her eyes lock with mine again. "I guess I'm asking for a little grace here. Maybe you're not as bad as I built you up to be in my head."

"See?"

"Cyrus," she reprimands when I smirk. "I let myself get carried away with you last night..." Her fingers twist in her lap, head dropping and voice small when she continues. "And I didn't hate it."

"I didn't hate it either, Antoinette." Her head snaps up at my words, so I press on. *It's now or never, Cy. Lay it all on the table.* "Actually, I'm rather fond of you, in case you hadn't noticed. If I told you I wanted to date you, what would you say?"

Brows shooting upward, she quickly schools her features before asking, "Do you think that's wise? We work together."

"Last I checked, the employee handbook doesn't say anything about relationships between employees."

"But—" Placing my fingers over her lips, I silence her. Flames lick the backs of her eyes, dancing among the gold of her irises.

Oh, she didn't like that.

I laugh under my breath before speaking again. "Just be quiet for one second, princess. Please. I like you, Antoinette. I want to learn more about you outside of the strong-willed, independent workaholic. I want to know what's in *here*." Moving my finger to her chest, I tap it against the warm skin over her heart. The organ inside thumps in a wild cadence against my palm when I flatten my hand. "Can you do that for me? Let me in. Let me know *you*. Not the corporate badass, but the *real* you." My voice drops to a whisper, and she leans closer, bracing her weight against my hand.

"I can try," she agrees softly, breath now mingling with mine as she cuts the distance between us. "Will you stay with me tonight?"

"On one condition." My tongue drags across my bottom lip. Her vertical pupils follow the movement as they blow wide.

A low moan vibrates out of her chest, gaze flicking up to mine. I take it as my cue to continue. "I'll stay... if you tell me something about yourself. Something about your childhood."

She started to open up earlier, and I want more.

I want all of her.

"Of course you'd make my request for your company conditional," she huffs, rolling her eyes.

Much to my dismay, she pulls back, leaving the bed and walking to the bathroom. The navy silk of her pants clings to her ass in the most tantalizing way. Washing over her supple cheeks with each step she takes away from me. At the door to the bathroom, she spins, challenge sparking in her gaze as she must catch me staring at her ass. "Fine. But I expect the same in return."

I groan and stretch out on the soft sheets of Antoinette's bed after stripping down to my boxer briefs. She said before, this is her nest. I see it now. There are piles of blankets in different soft textures, all scattered across the bed. A mountain of pillows in various sizes clutter the head of the bed. Not a bad place to sleep every night.

The temperature in the room is perfect... Not too hot or cold.

She hasn't pushed for anything sexual since I got here today, so I'm respecting her boundaries.

Plus, she seems... sad, like she could use a *friend,* not a fuck buddy.

Mags has told me in the past I'm a good listener—when I want to be. And right now, fuck, I want to be the best damn listener on the planet.

In the galaxy.

I want Antoinette to trust me.

I want to be a safe space for her.

The bathroom door swings open, her silhouette backlit by the dim light spilling through the doorway. Saliva pools in my mouth and my heart kicks up a notch, pumping all the blood south.

Suddenly, it's painfully obvious I'm going to have to work hard to keep my hands to myself until she makes the first move.

Clearing my throat, I pray my dick doesn't make a surprise entrance and ruin this rare unguarded moment between Antoinette and me.

Tucking an arm behind my head, I let my body melt into the mattress. "Damn, princess." I groan. "Your bed is very comfortable. I might have to sleep over more often."

The air is forced from my lungs when she chucks a pillow at my abdomen.

"Asshole. I'm regretting asking you to stay already. I can't believe I actually caved last night and had sex with you. You're incorrigible."

But I don't miss the slight lift at the corner of her mouth, or the sarcasm laced in her voice. Who knew she had a sense of humor?

"What can I say?" Waving my free hand down my body, I bounce my pec muscles a little. "The ladies find it hard to resist these godlike good looks."

Her white teeth glitter along with the fairy lights surrounding the bed. "And so modest, too." A clipped laugh rings through the air as she settles on her side next to me. "I'll admit, you're growing on me."

Flipping to my side, I reach out and tuck a strand of raven hair behind her ear. She turns into my touch, so I let my hand linger on the side of her neck. "Tell me what it's like to grow up as a dragon," I coax, hope sprouting in my chest, like a spring seedling, when she scoots closer.

"It was... lonely." Sadness seeps into her molten eyes, dimming their light ever-so-slightly. And I hate it. I want this powerful woman to burn as bright as the sun. I want her to have everything she desires. Which will hopefully include me someday.

Silence lingers between us, but I think she's gathering her thoughts. Eyes closed, she cups my hand to her cheek, like she needs my touch in order to speak. "Dragons are extremely rare and a solitary breed. I didn't have any siblings growing up, so it was just me and my mother. She was rather cold most of the time, like caring for me was a burden. As soon as I could fly on my own two wings, she quite literally kicked me out of the nest."

A fist clenches around my heart. How could a mother abandon their only child? And how long has Antoinette been alone? "How old were you?"

"Eighteen." She shrugs, like it's normal for a parent to kick you to the curb as a teenager. Those were some of the most important years with my parents before I lost them. My dad teaching Roman and me to drive. My mom fussing over me and my prom date when I was a senior in high school. The annual family vacations to the beach where we'd search for seashells during the day and laugh around the bonfire at night.

Antoinette's soft voice snaps me out of my happy memories, and I focus all my attention back on her. "I was eighteen the last time I saw my mother. Which was centuries ago."

"H-how old are you?"

Clicking in the silence, the clear membranes over her eyes close and open. "Two-hundred years old."

My mouth falls open, and I know I look ridiculous with my face frozen in shock. *Well, fuck me sideways.* She doesn't look a day over thirty. Illuminated by the moonlight, I let my eyes wander over her flawless tan skin. Smooth and inviting.

Midnight strands of thick, wavy hair spill across her pillow in a dark waterfall. She really is beautiful.

And when she smiles, like she is right now, my heart nearly stops beating. Twin fangs gleam in the low light, making my skin tingle and heat. A hearty chuckle drips from her throat. "Does that surprise you?"

With a surprisingly gentle touch, Antoinette uses a single finger under my chin to close my gaping mouth. A rush of warmth flows from the brief point of contact, making me crave more of her soft touches. "No offense, but you're stunning for being over two centuries old."

With a huffed laugh, she rolls her eyes, but they're laced with humor. "Wow, thanks."

All too soon, she drops her hand and tucks it back under the pillow her head rests on. It takes all my personal restraint not to reach out and cup her hand to my cheek.

I sober, remembering she was in the midst of bearing her past to me. "What about your dad? Wasn't he around?"

She shakes her head. "No. My father didn't stick around after I was born, which is common among our kind. Dragons come together to create a single offspring, so we don't go completely extinct, but the males aren't involved in raising the hatchling."

My fingers itch with the need to run through her silky black hair, where it cascades around her shoulders. But I resist, too afraid to disrupt the dialogue between us. "What did you do after your mother kicked you out? That was, what, one-hundred-eighty years ago?"

"Give or take." She shrugs. "Legends about dragons were still circulating around Europe at the time, so I was forced into hiding. Our species has been hunted throughout history because one bite from a dragon results in immortality for the recipient. You can imagine what people would do to become immortal."

In my chest, my heart slams against my ribs. "Holy shit, Antoinette. You were hunted?"

"Not me personally. No. But my mother told me horrible stories from her childhood, so I hid for nearly a century. In the 1920s, I caught wind of a boat headed for America, and I stowed away. Women were starting to gain more independence in the United States, so the timing was perfect. Don't get me wrong, I was still terrified of someone finding out I was a dragon, so I kept to myself. Living on the outskirts of society and gaining knowledge wherever I could. The libraries at NYU became some of my favorite places. And I would sneak into lectures whenever I could." Her golden eyes glaze over like she's remembering her time in the city when she first arrived.

"But you were still alone?" A wave of melancholy washes over me; I hate that she had no one.

She nods. "Yes. For about fifty years, I lived like that. Absorbing every morsel of knowledge. Working odd jobs to survive, but saving every spare cent for the future. When monsters finally came out and began living in the open alongside humans, I climbed the corporate ladder. I knew all the ins and outs of the city from my time here, so commercial properties seemed like a no-brainer."

My hand slides across the sheet between us, not touching her. But, damn, I want her in my arms more than anything. "Antoinette, I'm sorry you've been alone for so long."

"Meeting Penelope made everything so much better. She's been a godsend when it comes to managing my temper." A slow blush creeps across her cheeks, barely visible in the low glow of the fairy lights. "I don't know what I'd do without her. Sometimes I forget how to interact with others... human or monster, but she's helped immensely."

Sadness still lingers in her voice and the need to hold her, comfort her, wins out. I slide my hand around her waist, to her back, tugging her with me when I roll. We end up with her sprawled nearly on top of me, leg draped over my hip and her upper half nestled against my chest. It feels right. "I'm so sorry, Antoinette."

In the darkness, her eyes glow, like twin beacons in a raging storm, guiding me to the safety of her shore.

"It wasn't all bad," she reassures, voice soft in the quiet bedroom. "The past fifty years have been much better since monsters came out of hiding. There was some initial prejudice, but everything seems to have settled in recent decades."

She yawns. I'm sure she's exhausted from the emotional ups and downs of the day, so I decide to switch to a lighter subject. "So you said earlier, this is your nest or hoard or whatever. Why the exorbitant number of blankets and pillows?" I punch one of the pillows to my left, my fist sinking into the cloud-soft material.

"Dragon's hoard what they covet most. All my life, I've wanted closeness and companionship. It's not natural for a dragon to crave those things since we're inherently loners, so I created a cozy environment to meet my needs. It's stupid." She huffs, rubbing her face against my chest.

Curling my hand around her neck, I use my thumb to tip her head up until she meets my gaze. "It's not stupid.

This room fits you, Antoinette. And it's served its purpose until now, right?"

"I guess."

Looking deep into her eyes, I get lost in the fireworks of gold exploding in her gaze. "But maybe now you could let me be your comfort?"

Her throat bobs against my hand, and as the silence hangs in the air, eyes locked, I'm certain she'll say no.

"Can you be patient with me?"

"Always."

She nods. "I can try."

"That's all I ask, Antoinette. It's late. We should get some sleep." My lips meet her forehead in a soft kiss before I settle against my pillow. "Goodnight, princess."

A little contented sigh slips from her parted lips, and she nuzzles closer to my chest, the arm around my waist tightening, like she doesn't want to let me go. I'll do everything in my power to get more of this soft Antoinette, because this side is making me fall even harder.

And I'm pretty sure I'm already in too deep to give a damn.

A stupid grin is plastered on my face when I close my eyes and drift to sleep, with the woman of my dreams curled around me.

CHAPTER 17

Cyrus

Groaning, I blink my eyes open and come face to face with a smirking Antoinette. Still in her pajamas, face bare and silken strands of black hair brushing her shoulders, she reclines against a mountain of pillows.

In her hand is a purple mug that says *My Boss is Hotter Than Yours*. Must be a gag gift from Pen. Raising the mug to her lips, she takes a sip.

"You know, you're actually pretty adorable when you're asleep. Probably because you're quiet." The gold flecks in her eyes dance with humor above the rim of her mug, a smile playing at the corners of her full lips when she takes another sip.

Rubbing my eyes, I force myself awake. Clearing my throat, I roll to the side and prop onto one elbow. "Ha. Ha. Very funny. Is that coffee?" Sitting up, I snatch the mug from her hands and take a big gulp.

Bitter, warm liquid fills my mouth, and I immediately regret my decision to steal her mug. "Blech." The disgusting liquid dribbles back into the mug. "What the hell is that? It's foul!"

Stifling a laugh, she takes the mug and sets it on the nightstand. "That *was* my lavender chamomile tea. Until you spit your backwash into it. Thank you very much, Wilcox."

"*That's* what I've been bringing you the past few weeks. Tastes like flowery dirt. What's wrong with coffee?"

Trying, and failing, to get rid of the putrid taste, I wipe my mouth on the back of my hand.

"I don't like coffee. It makes my dragon jittery, like a million ants are crawling under my scales."

The mention of her dragon has my brain conjuring up images of the majestic creature with stunning black and gold scales. "Your dragon. So is it still you when you transform?"

She nods and I scoot closer, an invisible thread pulling me into her orbit. "Yes. It's still me. Does that scare you?" Her voice is soft, quiet, maybe even a little hesitant.

I shake my head because it doesn't scare me, even though it probably should. "No. I'm fairly certain you wouldn't kill me."

Her eyes flash beneath thick dark lashes. "I suppose I won't end you. Not yet, anyway. You have proven to be quite good at giving orgasms." That breathtaking smile tugs at her lips again, until she must give in, and her mouth splits with laughter.

"Who knew Antoinette Bauer had a sense of humor?" I lean in closer, tucking a flyaway strand of black silk behind her ear. Blood pumps to my groin, and I start thinking with my other head.

I want to kiss her.

Touch her.

Taste her.

The pointed tips of her tongue skate across her lower lip, adding to the need flowing through my veins.

"Speaking of orgasms," I breathe, dipping closer until I'm hovering over her, our faces mere inches apart. "I can't stop thinking about the other night. At the office. How fucking amazing your pussy was. I think I might be addicted already."

A flame of lust flickers across her eyes, heating my skin when she searches my face.

"I've been thinking about this tongue, too." Using my thumb, I pull down her bottom lip until her jaw falls slack.

The forks of her tongue peek out, running along either side of my thumb.

All I can think is how much I wish that was my cock.

Up and down, she strokes, putting me under her spell. "You know, now would be a perfect time to demonstrate what else you can do with this tongue."

Her tongue slips back into her mouth and she says, "You're forgetting something, Wilcox."

Eyebrows scrunching together, I'm not prepared for her brute strength when she flips us. Knocking all the air from my lungs, she lands on top of me. A gusted "W-Wha—" is all I manage before she's straddling my hips.

Do I feel a little bit exposed as I lie against the pillows in only my boxer briefs?

Damn right, I do.

But my cock has other thoughts, pressing against the thin confines of the fabric, seeking the warm wetness it knows is between Antoinette's beautiful thick thighs.

Claw-tipped fingers wrapping around my throat snap my attention back to Antoinette's face, her eyes blazing even brighter. "You forget that I'm in charge, Mr. Wilcox."

"Yes, ma'am." My words cut off on a groan as she grinds her silk-covered core down on my lap. The friction against my cock is perfect.

If she keeps going like this, I'm sure to come in my damn boxers.

There's a wicked glint in her eyes, telling me that just might be her plan.

Two can play that game, princess.

Scooting up against the pillows until I'm sitting, I grip her hips and pull her closer. "You might be in charge, princess. But I'm not coming until you do." I wink, snaking one hand down the back of her pajama bottoms until I grip the supple flesh of her ass.

She's so soft and smooth.

And so damn warm.

Iridescent scales on her cheekbones and arms glint in the early morning light. Her dragon is right under the surface, and she's never looked sexier.

Her sultry moan hits my ears when I slip my hand lower, down the cleft of her ass, past her puckered hole, until I'm met by her warm cunt. Is she into ass play? I'm dying to find out, but her wet pussy calls to my wandering fingers. "Damn, princess. You're already leaking for me."

"Yes, all for you, Cyrus," she moans.

Cyrus. Not Wilcox, or asshole, or any of the other creative names she's called me. My name on her lips shoots a lightning bolt of pleasure straight to my balls.

She doesn't cower under my filthy words. No, this woman throws them right back at me and takes control in her own hands.

Using the grip on my throat, she pulls my lips to hers for a heated kiss. Teeth clash and tongues duel. I fucking love this push and pull between us. Neither one of us wants to give up control until we explode together.

It's everything I've ever wanted.

When she pulls back, I'm panting. From the torturous roll of her hips against my aching cock. Or from the scorching kiss. I'm not really sure, but... "You better not stop, princess. That feels fucking incredible."

Focusing on my fingers, I slip two inside her tight opening. Pre-cum leaks from my cock as her ribbed channel stretches to accommodate a third finger, and she moans in my ear. "Fuck, Cyrus. Keep doing that. You're so good with your fingers."

Goosebumps rise on my skin when her sharp claws scrape along my scalp. She buries them in the back of my hair and tugs. *Hard*. The pinch of pain zips straight down my spine to my balls, another surge of pre-cum spilling from the tip of my cock.

I groan, head tipping back on the pillows. "Antoinette, I need you to come. I'm not gonna last much longer."

Fingers thrusting faster, I use my other hand to grip her hip. The silk of her pajamas glides along my skin as I rock her against me.

Panted breaths puff against the shell of my ear when she commands, "Then be a good boy and make me come."

The sultry rasp to her voice has me doubling down, and she lets out a long, low groan in my ear as her cunt locks around my fingers. Her honeyed juices drip down into the palm of my hand.

I can't wait to taste her.

Since the night in our office, I've been salivating for a drop of her sweet nectar.

The thought alone—along with a whispered "Good boy"—has me unloading in my boxer briefs. Eyes pinching shut, I blindly reach for the back of Antoinette's neck and capture her mouth with mine. My pleasured groans are swallowed by our kiss as wave after wave of orgasm rushes over me.

Her hips slow, eventually coming to a stop and her pussy muscles soften enough for me to remove my fingers.

Pulling back, I maintain eye contact when I bring my glistening fingers between us. "Look at that, princess. You must like me a little bit." A drop of her release slides down my finger, and I chase it with my tongue, moaning when the sweet flavor hits my tastebuds. There's a hint of a smoky undertone, like a toasted marshmallow. "I knew you'd taste perfect. Next time, maybe you'll let me eat straight from the source."

Raising an eyebrow, I grip her hips and pull her close.

Her lips hover over mine, spreading into a sultry smirk. "Only if you're a good boy."

If any other woman called me a good boy, especially during sex, my dick would be limp. But when Antoinette Bauer says it—no, purrs it—I nearly come on command.

A shrill ringtone bursts our bubble. Antoinette places a peck on my lips before climbing off my lap. Grabbing her phone from the nightstand, she silences it. "Come on, Prince Charming. We need to get ready for work."

Running a hand over my face, I sigh, sinking into the fluffy mound of pillows and blankets. It's tempting to just stay in her bed all day. "What time is it?" The sun is peeking out from behind a row of clouds outside.

She exits the bathroom, toothbrush in one hand, make-up brush in the other. Always multitasking, even at home. "Just after seven. Pen is holding down the fort until we get to the office. Better hurry, Wilcox. You wouldn't want to show up in yesterday's rumpled suit and bedhead." She winks before retreating into the bathroom again.

Shit. I need to swing home for a shower and new clothes.

Springing from the bed, I wince as my boxer briefs stick to my skin. The now cooled cum slides down my leg. *Gross.*

I grab my clothes and find the guest bathroom down the hall. After cleaning up the best I can and dressing in my clothes from yesterday, sans underwear, I meet Antoinette in the kitchen.

Her back is to me while she stirs another mug of tea. Guess I'll get my coffee on the way to the office.

She's dressed in a figure-hugging deep-plum pencil skirt, paired with a cream sleeveless silk blouse. Raven hair falls in a pin straight sheet to her shoulders. It ruffles when she spins to face me, a soft smile on her lips. Today, they're painted the same shade as her skirt, and all I can think is what that color would look like smeared on my—

Clearing my throat, I step in front of her. "Hey. Can I take you somewhere this weekend?"

Her eyebrows furrow.

I run my thumb between them, smoothing them back into place. "You shared some difficult things with me last night, and I believe I promised to do the same. I'd like to introduce you to the people I care about most. My family."

"Are you sure?"

I smile. "Yeah, princess. I'm sure."

Her smile matches my own when she says, "I'd really like that." But her face falls a second later.

"What's wrong?" I stroke my fingers down her cheek before cupping the side of her neck.

Like always, she's hot to the touch. And I crave the familiar warmth on my fingertips almost as much as I need air in my lungs.

"How do we handle this"—she points a finger from her to me—"at the office? I don't want people to know."

My gut drops, and it must show on my face because she clarifies. "Yet. I don't want people to know yet. I've worked hard to get where I am, Cyrus. I don't want the board to think less of me because the two of us are dating. Is that even what we're doing? This is all so new and it could fizzle out."

Cupping her cheeks, I direct her gaze to me. "Hey, breathe."

She sucks in a breath at the same time I do, then blows it out with me.

"This is new. You're right, but I'm committed, okay? I want you, and I'll go at whatever pace you need. So we'll keep things quiet at work. We both know Penelope won't say anything. I'll be good and keep my hands to myself at the office. Okay?"

One fang sinks into her plump lower lip, and she nods. "Thank you." Another shrill ringtone sounds from behind her.

Spinning, she grabs the phone and swipes her finger across the screen before saying, "We're really behind now. Go home and shower. I'll meet you at work."

Since I know I won't be able to touch her for the next eight to ten hours, I wrap a hand around her throat and tug her mouth to mine for one more drugging kiss. Then I speed home for the world's fastest shower so I can spend the rest of the day cataloging each expression that crosses her beautiful face.

Yeah, I've got it bad.

CHAPTER 18

Antoinette

True to his word, Cyrus has kept his distance over the past few days. But I don't miss the way his eyes linger on me, especially my ass, every chance he gets. And when we happen to be in the break room or copy room alone together, he makes sure to invade my space until I'm surrounded by a wall of his cologne. The hint of vanilla has my insides turning into a knotted mess.

It's like I'm a blushing schoolgirl and my legs turn to jelly every time he brushes his fingers against mine. The hint of warmth from his skin sets a swarm of dragonflies loose in my gut.

I'm not this woman. I don't swoon over men—yet here I am.

One thing's for sure, I can't deny my growing feelings for Cyrus any longer.

Even now, his cerulean stare burns my skin from across the conference room table, pulling my attention from Mr. Andrews, who drones on and on about his extravagant weekend plans in the Hamptons. Must be nice.

"That sounds lovely, sir. I hope the weather cooperates for you," I say, winking at Cyrus before I swing my head toward our boss.

"You just never know this time of year. Now, I have a tee time with my brother in a half hour, so why don't you give me an update on your current project?" His eyes swing expectantly toward Cyrus.

Once again, Andrews shows his true colors, defaulting to Cyrus, simply because he has a dick between his thighs. Heat bubbles from my core—and not the good kind, the kind born from anger.

Just a little longer, I remind myself. A few more commission bonuses and I'll be able to afford the startup costs for my own firm. I'll finally be my own boss.

Unblinking, Cyrus locks eyes with me. "Actually, Ms. Bauer has been spearheading this project. What she's come up with is spectacular, and I think you'll be impressed."

Cyrus's words settle some of the previous irritation trickling through me. "Thank you, Cyrus."

"And everything is on schedule? The board expects a presentation at the end of the month." Mr. Andrews cuts his beady eyes toward me, gleaming with condescension.

I sit up straighter, rolling my shoulders back. "Yes. As soon as the client accepts our offer, we're ready to move forward, sir."

His face turns an unnatural shade of red that has my hackles rising. "You haven't secured the property yet! This is a rookie mistake, Antoinette. Not something I'd expect to see from a seasoned agent, such as yourself."

"Sir, he's—"

He holds up a hand, silencing me and adding fuel to the anger in my veins.

I hate being interrupted.

"Fix it, Antoinette. Or you won't have a job here anymore." With a final glare, he stands from his chair. "Don't fuck it up, Ms. Bauer. I took a chance on you before; I won't do it again."

A curt nod to Cyrus, and he's gone, the conference room door slamming shut behind him.

All I see is red; it bleeds into my periphery and clouds my field of vision. Under my skin, my dragon uncurls and scales break through the surface.

In a rage-fueled blur, my feet carry me to my office. Voices echo around me, but they're muffled, like I'm underwater.

Grabbing the first thing I can—a stack of papers on my desk—I swipe them on the floor. A few sheets burst into flames from my heated touch.

Before I can reach for the poor potted plant on the corner of my desk, heavy hands latch onto my shoulders and spin me. "Princess, stop." The glacial blue of his eyes douses the inferno inside me instantly.

How does he do that? How does he calm my inner dragon with a single touch? A single look?

"Talk to me, Antoinette. Let me in—please." His voice is soft and soothing as he leans his forehead against mine.

A lesser man would be afraid; my blazing eyes, the smoke swirling around us, and my skin is hotter than lava. But not Cyrus. His inner strength shines through in these moments when it's just the two of us.

I promised I would try to let him in, even if it's hard. Time to make good on that promise. Blowing out a breath, I draw my strength from him, focusing on the ring of dark navy surrounding his pupils. "I've had to fight every day to get where I am in my career. So when he doubts me... or overlooks me because I'm a woman, it makes me furious."

He nods, big hands coming up to cup my face. "I'm not going to pretend to understand what you've been through, princess. And I'm sorry if I was a chauvinistic asshole at any point in the past. But I promise I'll be by your side through all the ups and downs. Okay?"

Licking my suddenly dry lips, I nod. "Yeah. And thank you for sticking up for me. Your words meant a lot in there, even if they rolled right off Mr. Andrews's back."

"You're welcome. He's an asshole. And he's always given me the creeps. His brother's even worse." His large frame shudders and he pinches his eyes shut. When they open again, there's heat behind them. "Thank you for letting me in, Antoinette. I know it's not easy. And maybe I can help relieve some of the tension."

Peeling away from me, his mouth breaks into a lopsided grin as he approaches the door to our office. "Hey, Pen!"

Penelope appears in the doorway a second later. "Yes, Cy."

Pulling out his wallet, he slips his credit card from its slot and hands it to her. "Can you grab the three of us some lunch? How about that new bistro that opened down the street? Get a few options... and take your time."

Credit card in hand, she scampers away, and Cyrus closes the door, clicking the lock into place.

"What are you up to, Mr. Wilcox?" The rasp in my voice floats across the quiet office.

Cyrus pulls the cord on the blinds of the door, effectively shielding us from prying eyes. There's a wicked glint in his pale eyes when he turns toward me and stalks across the tile floor. Somehow, he appears larger, broad shoulders threatening to pop the seams of his suit jacket.

Bracing my butt against the edge of my desk, I tip my head back, maintaining eye contact as he comes to stand in front of me.

He towers over me, reminding me there's a significant difference in our heights. Even if I do have the advantage of being a shifter, he still has at least eight inches on me.

Hands braced on either side of my hips, he leans in close, minty breath heating the side of my face when he growls, "I know we said we'd keep this quiet at work, but you need to relax. And I know just how to help, princess."

I'm almost ashamed to admit the wanton sound that tumbles from my throat when his fingers slip to the hem of my dress. Ever-so-slowly, his rough hands slide the flowing material up until the red satin between my thighs is on full display.

I moan, knowing exactly where this is headed. But nerves wiggle their way into the back of my mind. "What if someone comes looking for us?"

Fingers digging into the fat at my hips, he boosts me onto the desk. "The door's locked, and that was our last meeting for the day." The gravel in his voice has a trickle of arousal coating my panties. "I know you like to be in charge, Antoinette, but it's my turn now. Do you understand?"

I shake my head, resisting the urge to submit. "Fuck you, Cyrus." The hissed words turn into a moan when he glides a thumb over the front of my panties, pressing down on my clit.

"No, princess. I'll be the one fucking you right now." His thick fingers hook in the sides of the scrap of fabric and glide it down my legs. My jaw falls slack when he brings the balled-up ruby fabric to his nose and sucks in a breath. "Damn, you're delicious."

I know for a fact I'm not getting that pair back when he shoves them in the pocket of his slacks, a wolfish smirk on his handsome face.

Wetness trails down my inner thighs as he continues to toy with me, running a finger around my opening, but never breaching me. *Asshole.*

"Wilcox, stop teasing and make me come." I rock my hips forward, chasing his touch.

His chuckle melts over my skin like warm butter. At this point—his torturous fingers still circling my clit, never venturing where I want them most—my words are all bark and no bite.

Blunt teeth nip at my neck, then my earlobe, before he whispers, "Turn your brain off and come on my tongue. Can you be a good little dragon and do that for me?"

My hands skim over the thick material of his jacket, the wool rough against my palms. Shoving it off his shoulders and arms, the heavy garment thuds to the floor. "Then get on your knees for me, Cyrus. Make my pussy gush for you.

Can *you* be a good boy and do that for me?" Smirking, I throw his words back at him.

His answering groan ripples through me, zipping straight to my clit as he lowers to his knees. Under the thin white cotton of his dress shirt, the corded muscles of his arms flex and roll, causing more honey to leak from my aching cunt.

Those warm hands coast up my legs, latching onto my knees and spreading me wide, making room for his impossibly broad shoulders. The look on his face is that of a man possessed, starved, and feral. A lock of dark-blonde hair falls over one eyebrow as he licks his lips and leans closer.

Giving in to my baser needs, I stroke a hand through the thick strands and clutch the roots, guiding him closer to the source of his desires. "You do look rather good on your knees, Wilcox. Now put your tongue where it belongs."

Cupping his cheek, I give it a light smack and he growls, deep and low in his chest. His gaze is otherworldly, nearly glowing with lust as he peers up from between my spread thighs.

He's fucking perfect, this man I've waited two-hundred years for.

The first lap of his tongue has my fingers tightening in his hair and my back arching. Hard as diamonds, my nipples scrape against the lace of my bra, and I wish, more than anything, we were both naked and in the sanctuary of my nest right now.

But as Cyrus swirls his tongue around my clit, all coherent thoughts are wiped from my brain. Helpless to my own lust, all I can do is mewl and whimper when he thrusts the thick muscle deep into my pussy. The inner, ribbed walls give way, making room for him to eat to his heart's content.

"Cyrus, yes," I sigh, bracing my free hand behind me. I use the leverage to roll my hips against his face. His nose nuzzles my clit, sending a shock wave through me. I'm not going to last much longer. "Right there."

Ever the good boy, Cyrus takes direction well and continues to feast, licking up every drop of my arousal as it leaks from me. Replacing his nose with his thumb, he strums vigorously at my clit until my toes curl inside my red-soled stilettos. His moans of ecstasy vibrate against my core, only heightening my own pleasure as I slingshot into orgasm.

"Yes, Cyrus!" I scream, tugging on his hair, not caring if I suffocate him with my flesh. All I care about is prolonging my own euphoria as my hips roll against his face, riding out the last wave until my fingers and toes tingle.

Once my muscles relax, my eyes spring open, heart fluttering like hummingbird wings in my chest. "Do you think anyone heard me?"

Standing before me, Cyrus wipes around his mouth with his fingers before sucking them between his lips, moaning loudly. One glance at the obvious bulge in the front of his pants makes his own need blatantly clear. His eyes open, still burning with lust, and he smirks. "Do you really care?"

I scoff, shoving his chest, but he catches my wrist and tugs me to him. Our mouths crash together, and I whimper, tasting the tangy nectar of my own release on his tongue. "Yes, I care," I mumble between kisses. "I don't want people to think I slept my way to the top."

When we break apart, there's a hint of sadness in his eyes. "Shit, princess, I didn't even think of that. You were tense and angry. I was just trying to take the edge off and distract you."

I smile at the sincerity in his tone. "I know, Cyrus. And I don't blame you for what others may think. Plus, I do feel better. You, however, seem to have a problem." I point at the erection straining against his zipper.

Pink bursts onto his cheeks and the tips of his ears. *Cute.*

He runs his fingers through his now messy hair, trying to comb the strands back into place. "This was about you, Antoinette. Not me. Although, I wouldn't say no if you wanted to repay the favor tomorrow night."

His salacious wink has my cheeks heating.

"On our mystery date?"

He laughs, probably at the confusion on my face. He's told me next to nothing about where he's taking me this weekend, besides the fact he's introducing me to his family.

And to pack a bag, specifically casual attire.

To say I'm stressed is an understatement.

On cue, the familiar nerves I've become friends with since letting Cyrus behind my walls push their way to the front of my mind.

This is the first time I've actually dated someone. None of my past flings have been serious enough to warrant much more than a warm body on a cold night.

I've never had someone take me away for a weekend, let alone meet their family. What if I say the wrong thing? What if they don't like me?

I know I can come off cold and standoffish.

"Penny for your thoughts." Wrapping his arms around me, Cyrus pulls me against his chest. The fabric of my dress falls down to cover my lower half when I stand. Leaning my head between his firm pec muscles, his heart beats rapidly against my ear, soothing my frazzled nerves.

Tipping my head back, I meet his gaze, shocked by the simmering emotion shining through. "I'm just nervous, I guess."

He strokes a finger along my jaw, swiping the tip under my bottom lip as he speaks in a quiet voice. "Don't be. They're going to see how amazing you are the second they meet you. Okay?"

I nod, but before our conversation can go any further, there's a soft knock at the door. Probably Penelope with our food, and I reluctantly pull out of his warm embrace.

He flashes me a smile over his shoulder while he unlocks the door, letting Pen into the office.

My cheeks heat, the flush trailing down my neck and chest when she winks at me, heading to the conference table in the corner of the office with three large bags of food.

"You buy the whole place, Pen?" Cyrus teases.

She giggles, taking multiple Styrofoam to-go containers out of the bags. "You said to get a few different options. Just following orders, boss man."

As I lean against my desk, I let their playful back-and-forth hum around me, filling my heart until it's ready to overflow. I'm finally not alone and it's everything I've always wanted.

Hopefully, after this weekend, my family will grow even bigger... all thanks to the asshole staring at me with twinkling blue eyes. "You coming, princess?"

Pushing off my desk, I cross the room toward what I hope is my future.

CHAPTER 19

Antoinette

My phone skitters across the bathroom vanity as I apply a final coat of mascara on my lashes. "Shoot!" I hiss when the wand hits my lid, leaving a smudged trail of burgundy in its wake.

Screwing the lid shut, I set the mascara tube in my makeup bag and grab the vibrating phone. My thumb swipes across the screen, answering the call before I stuff my phone between my shoulder and ear. "Hello?"

"Hey, princess." Cyrus's husky voice filters down the line, setting my pulse into a frenzy.

Eyes flicking to the mirror, I find my cheeks blushed a rosy red and a dopey smile on my lips. The subtle burgundy of my eyeliner and mascara brings out the gold of my eyes as they twinkle back at me. I almost don't recognize this *happy* version of myself, but she's starting to show up more and more since I let Cyrus into my life.

"Cat got your tongue, Antoinette? Or did hearing my voice take your breath away?" He chuckles.

I shake my head at his lame joke and grab a cotton swab from the container on the countertop. "Asshole. No. I was finishing my makeup, and your phone call made me get mascara all over my eyelid." Flipping on the faucet, I wet the end of the cotton swab and run it over the dried mascara. *There. Good as new.* "Are you here already?"

A car door slams, followed by some muffled noises. "Yeah, I'm parked in the visitor spot by the front door. Are you sure you don't want me to come up? I'm a gentleman, princess. Let me feel useful and carry your bag."

Makeup fixed, I toss the dirty cotton swab into the trash and grab my makeup bag before turning off the light and entering my bedroom. "I'm a big girl; I can carry my own bag, Cyrus. I'll be down in a few minutes."

"You packed casual clothes, right?"

Rolling my eyes, I toss the makeup bag into my tan-colored weekender tote and zip it shut. "Yes, Cyrus. I do own jeans, you know?"

A pained groan hits my ears. "Fuck, princess. I love seeing you in your boss babe uniform, but I can't wait to see you in some skintight denim."

Turning toward the full-length mirror hanging on the wall, I do a quick spin, smiling when my eyes land on the dark denim hugging my ass. *Yeah, he's going to lose his ever-loving mind.* Paired with a cream cashmere V-neck sweater and burgundy ankle boots, I'm the picture of casual—okay, elevated casual. Can't blame a girl for liking nice things. "How ever will you contain yourself?" I snark, hoisting the straps of my bag over one shoulder and draping my khaki trench coat over my arm. "Keep it in your pants until later. Okay, Wilcox? I want to make a good impression. I don't need you pawing at me all day."

In reality, my confidence is at an all-time high under his lingering touches and heated stares.

But I do want his family to like me. He hasn't told me anything about them, so I have no idea what kind of situation he's dragging me into.

"I'll be on my best behavior, Ms. Bauer. Just get your sexy ass down here, because I won't be held responsible for my actions if I have to come up there." There's no real threat behind his words, only the same sarcastic taunt I've become all too familiar with over the past few weeks.

"I'm heading down now. Goodbye, Cyrus." Not giving him a chance to get the last word, I hang up and slip the phone into my back pocket. Making sure all the lights are off, I grab my purse and keys before locking the door and heading for the elevator. All the while, the same dopey, love-struck grin remains securely fixed on my face.

Brilliant crimson and yellow leaves dance across the blacktop as we barrel down the two-lane highway, heading north, away from the city. My eyes are glued out the passenger window, nose nearly pressed against the glass, as I take in the beautiful surroundings. "It's breathtaking," I whisper, gaze lingering on the bright red maples lining the roadway.

I'd nearly forgotten how the leaves swoop and flutter, floating on the gentle breeze before landing on the ground.

Normally, I'm the one soaring *above* the treetops, and any falling leaves are mere specks in my periphery.

"When's the last time you left the city, princess? You're acting like a kid in a candy store over there." He chuckles at my expense, but I'm too wrapped up in the autumnal surroundings and the warmth of his laughter to care.

"I'll admit, it's been a while. I don't lead a very exciting life, so sue me," I bristle, eyes still firmly fixed out my window.

Lately, every free second has been spent focusing on the O'Malley project and making sure every detail is perfect in preparation for our presentation to the board. I can't afford to fuck things up and lose this job. I've finally made it to the top.

I don't plan on having it all taken away. No. My plan is to leave on my own terms when I'm finally ready to start my own firm.

Suddenly, a heavy hand lands on my thigh, squeezing until I turn and latch onto his cool gaze. "We're about to change that. No more weekends at the office. No more nights spent alone. You feel me, princess?"

Throat thick with emotion, I don't trust myself to speak, so I simply nod and let a smile break free.

"That's better," he says. "Happiness looks good on you, Antoinette."

Heat warms my cheeks, and I pull away from his penetrating stare, content to spend the rest of the journey enamored by the fall foliage. I've spent so much of my life hiding or struggling to get to the next rung on the corporate ladder that I've forgotten the simple joys—like a scenic truck ride with a boyfriend.

Is that what he is?

Is Cyrus Wilcox my *boyfriend?*

The word is foreign as it ping-pongs around my brain until I can't keep it inside anymore.

Slicing my gaze back to him, I blurt my question. "Are you my boyfriend?"

The corners of his mouth twitch, like he's trying—and failing—to hold back a smirk. Not even a second later, his lips split to reveal a perfect white smile. "Do you want me to be your boyfriend, Antoinette?"

I shrug, looking out the windshield. "I-I guess I never really thought about it. It does feel a little juvenile, though. Don't you think? I mean, I'm over two-hundred years old and you're almost forty."

"Hey! Don't throw me over the hill quite yet. I'm only thirty-eight. But I don't look a day over twenty-five." Dark-blonde eyebrows waggle, the wrinkles at the corners of his eyes more prominent in the late afternoon sunlight.

True, he doesn't look his age, but he sure as hell doesn't look like a man in his twenties.

Rolling my eyes, I place my hand over his on my thigh. I like the way it feels, to touch him freely and have him do the same. I've always craved physical contact, having been deprived of it most of my life. "Age? That's what you're hung up on?"

"Okay, okay." He squeezes my thigh again, and I resist the urge to press my legs together. Seems like every time I'm around Cyrus, there's a low ache in my core, and I've come to crave it. "What if you're just *mine* and I'm *yours*?"

My brow furrows. Is it really that easy? "Is that enough?"

"Enough? Antoinette, I don't think you've quite grasped the situation yet. Let me help you catch up. I'm in this to the end. I don't want another woman. I only want *you*. Forever." His eyes meet mine, serious and sure.

"You don't—You can't mean that?" My stomach twists, tightening with the fear of rejection. My own parents didn't want me; why would this man? This beautiful, stubborn, arrogant man.

"Let's get one thing straight, princess. When I say something, I mean it. Don't try to change my mind. So, you're mine and I'm yours. Say it back for me."

And I do. Lacing my fingers with his, I repeat the words and maybe, just maybe, let myself believe them... for now, at least. "You're mine and I'm yours." My heart soars, that dopey smile on my face as Cyrus pulls the truck onto a long gravel driveway lined on both sides by rows and rows of apple trees.

Slowing to a crawl, we approach a sprawling white farmhouse with a wraparound porch and a candy apple red front door. Color me intrigued. "So this is where you hide every Sunday."

Cranking the gearshift into park, Cyrus turns toward me, clasping both of my hands between his much larger ones. His warmth radiates up my arms, straight to my pounding heart. "This is my favorite place because two of the most important people in the world live here. Are you ready to meet my little family, princess?"

The sincerity in his cerulean eyes has me swallowing around a lump in my throat. "Yes," I whisper, his earlier claiming giving me the confidence I need.

Suddenly, the jokester is back, his face morphing into a lopsided smirk. My panties don't stand a chance as he swings his door open and jumps out of the truck, calling over his shoulder, "This time, I'm carrying the bags."

I'm still chuckling by the time I climb out of the truck and make my way to the bed. True to his words, Cyrus has a bag slung over each shoulder and a small stuffed unicorn in his hands that I hadn't noticed earlier.

The sight of the tiny plush toy has dragonflies breaking free to swarm my stomach.

You can do this, Antoinette. You meet new people all the time for your job. Yeah, but they're not important to the person I love.

Love?

Is that what this is? Why my heart is ready to rip out of my chest and my armpits won't stop sweating? Or why I want to be around this man I once hated?

No.

It's too soon.

I won't let my brain or my heart fall for Cyrus Wilcox just yet. I won't give him the power to hurt me again.

"This is the main house, but we'll be staying in the guest house at the back of the property." He points to a small cabin barely visible through the rows of trees. "It's far enough away from the main house to give us a little privacy. I'll drop our bags there once I introduce you to Maggie and Lily. Ready?" he asks, peering over his shoulder.

I nod and follow him toward the quaint farmhouse. Around us, the leaves rustle in the wind and the birds twitter, soaking up the warm rays of autumn sunshine.

As we approach the porch steps, something in the window catches my eye. A little girl, maybe five or six, has her nose squished to the glass, a beaming smile on her cherubim face. Her blonde hair is pulled into two pigtails, the curly ends bouncing down to her shoulders.

She doesn't really bear any resemblance to the man in front of me. Who is this sweet little girl?

"They're here! They're here!" Her muffled voice meets my ears before she disappears from sight.

The red front door swings open to reveal a petite, curvy woman with the same curly blonde hair and pale-green eyes as the little girl. If I had to guess, this must be her mother.

Cyrus climbs the steps and dumps our bags unceremoniously on the wooden front porch. I stand next to him, awkwardly twisting my sweaty hands in the shoulder strap of my purse. A storm rages in my gut and I'm not sure if I'm going to vomit on my shoes or turn tail and run.

I've never been this nervous in my life.

The little girl appears a moment later, arms wrapped around the woman's hips as she beams up at me and Cyrus. Her little body is practically vibrating with excitement, wiggling against her mother's side.

I can't help but smile. Her enthusiasm eases some of the tension within my muscles. I have a feeling I'm going to like this little girl.

"Uncle Cy!" Detaching herself from the woman, the little girl dive bombs at Cyrus. He lets out an *oomph* when she collides with him, wrapping her arms around his trim waist.

Nerves forgotten, I giggle when he plants one foot behind him, catching his balance before scooping the pint-sized renegade into his arms. "Hi, Lily Bear. Long time no see."

"It's only been a week," she huffs, smashing his cheeks between her little hands. "Is that for me?" Big eyes swing to the stuffed unicorn somehow still clutched in Cyrus's grip.

He hums, mouth pursing to the side. "I don't know. Do you know anyone around here who *loves* unicorns?"

Tugging the toy from his grasp, the little girl squeals. "I do! I do! Thank you, Uncle Cy!"

A throat clears to my left, and Cyrus's eyes widen. "Oh, right. Maggie, this is Antoinette Bauer." He sweeps his free hand toward me while keeping the little girl, Lily, tucked safely in his other arm. "Princess, this is my sister-in-law, Maggie Wilcox."

Sister-in-law? Cyrus has never mentioned a brother. In fact, he hasn't really mentioned anything about his family. I wonder why.

Remembering my manners, I extend a hand toward Maggie. Subtly wiping the sweat on the thigh of my jeans first because no one likes a clammy handshake. *Gross.*

A very unattractive squeak falls from my mouth when she blows right past my hand, wrapping me in a warm bear hug instead. The scent of fresh apples wafts off her hair, the curly strands tickling my nose when she pulls back.

Bracing both hands on my shoulders, she squeezes gently and peers up at me. Her voice is soft and gentle when she says, "We're huggers in this family. Hope that's okay."

I nod. "Yes. Yeah." I've never been much for hugs, but Maggie's arms around me felt right. Like a long-lost friend or sister.

Wide-eyed, I swing toward Cyrus, who smiles and tips his head. Now that he's side by side with his niece, I see the resemblance. They have the same lip shape, both currently in wide smiles. And, upon closer inspection, Lily's hair is actually the same dirty-blonde shade as his.

"And who's this little ball of energy?" I ask, eyes glued to the wiggling child in Cyrus's arms. From the soft expression on his face, it's clear he'd give anything for this little girl.

A giggle bursts from her mouth when Cyrus tickles her side, her face turning red as she gasps for air. "This is Lily, my favorite niece."

Once she's caught her breath, Lily's tiny eyebrows pull together, furrowing in the middle. "Momma, are there other nieces?"

Stifling a laugh behind her hand, Maggie's eyes bounce between Lily and Cyrus. "No, Lil. You're the only niece. Uncle Cy is just pulling your leg."

"Not my legs!" she screeches, clutching at her little knobby knees through her rainbow print leggings. "That's not very nice, Uncle Cy." The cutest scowl mars her face, and I bite my lip to stop from laughing, because something tells me this is a very serious matter to her.

Pulling her in for a big hug, Cyrus rubs her back, voice soft and sincere. "I'm sorry, Lily Bear. I was only joking. But you are my favorite."

A gust of wind ruffles my hair, sending a shiver down my spine. Maggie must notice because she picks up my bag and motions toward the door. "Where are my manners? Come inside, and we can get to know each other before dinner."

I smile, following her inside the old farmhouse. Stuffed toy in hand, Lily speeds ahead, chattering about a unicorn movie she watched last night, and Cyrus trails behind me with his bag slung over his shoulder.

Peering over my shoulder, I smile softly, matching the expression on his face as our eyes meet. Somehow, being surrounded by his favorite people in one of his favorite places, it's like I'm finally coming home for the first time in my life.

CHAPTER 20

Antoinette

L ater in the evening, we sit around the kitchen table, enjoying Maggie's cooking. Living on my own for most of my life, I'm not used to home-cooked meals like this. I nearly moan as I chew another bite of roast beef and mashed potatoes. This might be my new comfort food.

"This is really delicious, Maggie. Thank you for cooking." In my lap, my fingers twist in the cloth napkin. All day, Maggie has been nothing but kind and gracious, something I'm not entirely used to.

Maggie smiles. "You're welcome. We're happy to finally meet you. Cyrus has told me so much about you; I feel like I already know you."

My head whips to my right, toward Cyrus. *He told his sister-in-law about me?* Those all too familiar dragonflies break free from their cage again, swarming my tummy.

"All good things, I hope," I say, eyes glued to Cyrus, waiting for a clue as to what he's told Maggie. Right on cue, the tips of his ears redden to match his sculpted cheeks.

He clears his throat, but Maggie speaks first, putting him out of his misery. "Nothing bad. Don't worry." She winks before taking another bite of her food.

A tug at the left sleeve of my sweater has me looking down. Lily's hand is clutched in the soft material. "I really like your shirt. And your boots. You're really pretty."

My cheeks heat. It's not that I'm not used to being complimented, but it doesn't usually come from a small child. So I'm not entirely sure how to respond. "Um, thank you, Lily. That's very nice of you. I really like your... leggings."

Her eyes nearly double in size, the green in her irises shining bright. "You do?"

I nod, eyes skimming over the vibrant print encasing her legs. "I love rainbows, especially the purples and blues."

"Rainbows are my favorite, too." One of her front teeth is missing, making her smile even more endearing and adorable. "Momma said you're a dragon! Like in my books? Can you fly? And breathe fire? Can I see?" She bounces in her seat.

"Liliana Marie!" Maggie's raised voice comes from across the table, and both Lily and I turn toward her.

"What?" Lily whines.

"You can't go around asking people personal questions like that."

"Oh, it's fine," I say, hoping to deescalate the situation. "I don't mind. Dragons are rare, so most people don't know much about them."

Maggie picks up her fork again. "As long as you don't mind. Lily doesn't really have a filter yet, so she likes to ask inappropriate questions *a lot*. We're working on it. Right, Lily Bug?"

"Right, Momma!" Smile back in place, it's like she was never scolded. Peeking over at me beneath her thick lashes, she lowers her voice. "So can you fly?"

I burst out laughing. Lily might be my favorite, too. "Yes, I can fly."

"What does your dragon look like? Can I draw you?"

"Lily!" Maggie scolds again.

"Sorry, Momma." Turning to me, she says, "Sorry, Antoinette."

"It's okay. And you can call me Annie." I smile, patting her leg. "How about I give you a little Dragon 101?" I offer, folding my napkin and placing it on the table next to my plate.

Lily's eyebrows scrunch. "What does that mean?"

I hum, forgetting she's only five and doesn't understand everything. How can I explain things in her terms? "Are you in school?"

Her head bobbles with a nod. "Yeah! I love school!"

I smile. "Okay. So, like in school, you have math lessons or reading lessons. Well, how about I give you a quick lesson on dragons?"

"Okay!" Sea glass-green eyes light up, dinner totally forgotten.

Across from me, Maggie is smiling, eyebrows raised expectantly. And Cyrus's gaze shimmers with an emotion I'm not ready to face yet, like he can see me fitting in with his family for years to come.

Ignoring the cocktail of hope, fear, and love churning in my gut, I focus back on Lily and something I can control—teaching her the facts about dragons. "Okay, Miss Lily. Get ready to learn about dragons."

She squeals, and I launch into the basics of shifting, flying, and breathing fire. All the while, Cyrus's cerulean eyes nearly melt my skin with how intently he's watching me.

I think I'm out of my depth, and I don't know whether to dive in headfirst or run for the hills.

My heart is screaming, telling me to take the risk and fall, let Cyrus catch me with open arms.

But my head is telling me it's too soon.

It's too much.

He hurt me before. He could do it again.

The plate rattles against the drying rack when I set it down. Turning off the water, I wipe my hands on the dish towel next to the sink.

"You didn't have to do the dishes." The deep voice rumbles in my ear and my skin erupts with tingles as his lips brush the shell.

Leaning against the hard wall of his body, I let Cyrus's dark vanilla scent wrap around me while he hugs me close. Warm hands rest against the curve of my stomach, where it presses against the denim of my jeans. "I felt bad since Maggie cooked. It's the least I can do to help out." A breathy moan works its way up my throat when Cyrus brushes his lips against the side of my neck.

Sobering, I spin to face him, bracing my butt against the counter. As I swallow, my tongue is like sandpaper stuck against the roof of my mouth. "Do you think they like me?" I wince at how needy my voice is.

I'm not this person.

Usually, I don't give a flying fuck what others think of me.

But I'm starting to realize, Cyrus is important to me, so it's important that Maggie and Lily like me.

The wry smile melts off his handsome face, and he pulls me against his chest. I relish the steady drumbeat of his heart and the soothing warmth radiating from him. "Are you kidding, princess? Maggie loves you. And I think you're Lily's new role model. Before bed, she told me she wants to be a dragon when she grows up."

Foreign wetness coats the rims of my eyes. I sniffle, subtly rubbing my face against the worn fabric of his gray t-shirt before I pull back. Cyrus cups my cheek, thumb stroking under my eye and wiping away any stray moisture.

"She's amazing," I say, running my hands over his chest until they meet at the back of his neck. "If I was going to have kids, I'd want them to be just like Lily. So much enthusiasm for life packed into an adorable little package."

Before my eyes, his face morphs into a wry smile. "Finally, something we agree on, princess. I don't see myself ever having kids of my own. Lily is all I need. She's what kept me going after my brother died." His voice lowers, serious and somber.

Reaching a hand up, I cup his strong jaw, the stubble rough against my palm. In a low whisper, I ask, "Will you tell me about him?" I hold my breath, hoping he'll let me in.

Sadness flickers across his face. Gripping my hands, he pulls me toward the back door. "Yeah, but not here. Let's go for a walk. The orchard is magical this time of day."

The brisk fall air ruffles my hair as we walk through the rows of apple trees. Tugging my trench coat tighter around me, I try to stave off the biting evening chill. Even for a hot-blooded dragon shifter like myself, the October breeze has goosebumps rising on my arms.

But Cyrus is there, anticipating my every need. His fingers lace through mine, heat radiating up my arm from our joined hands.

A hint of sweetness wafts through the air, evidence of the remaining apples weighing down the branches of the trees surrounding us. Yellow and red leaves flutter to the ground with each gust of wind, and I bundle closer to Cyrus.

We walk in silence for a bit. His mind is probably racing from our earlier conversation in the kitchen. I don't know the whole story yet, or the level of grief he's dealing with, so I let the silence hang between us until he's ready.

Once we've been walking for a few minutes, he blows out a sigh. The hand clutching mine is slightly clammy, so I give his fingers a reassuring squeeze.

"I had a brother," he rasps, the words almost lost to the wind.

Had. Past tense. An invisible fist clenches around my heart, nausea looming close behind.

The sun sinks behind the treetops, casting a golden glow on Cyrus's profile. "He was my shadow growing up. Wherever I went, Roman went, too. When I started playing football, so did Roman." The blue in his eyes is like an ocean, crashing with waves of grief. His lips pull into a watery smile. "He was three years younger than me, and we were inseparable. Then he met Maggie, and it became the three of us against the world. When I graduated college and started working in the city, we drifted apart. Something I'll regret for the rest of my life."

This time, I squeeze his hand for my own comfort, swallowing over a dry spot in my throat. "What happened to him?"

"This place was his dream." Moisture shines in his eyes. Letting go of my hand, he spins in a circle, taking in the trees around us. "Roman never wanted to be a city slicker like me. No. He preferred the quieter life out here. He'd bought this place for a steal when they found out Mags was pregnant with Lily. He was so excited to spend his life out in the fresh air and sunshine." He's smiling, but it doesn't meet his eyes, and his voice wobbles when he continues. "A few years ago, at the start of harvest season, Roman said goodbye to Maggie and Lily in the morning, going out for his routine check on the workers and the trees, but he never came home. One of the workers found him." The thick muscles in his neck constrict when he swallows. "He died of a brain aneurysm that we never even knew was there."

Some instinct deep in me takes over, and I collide with Cyrus, wrapping my arms around him in a suffocating embrace. My eyes well with tears, and I choke out, "I'm so sorry, Cyrus. You don't have to keep going if it's too much. I understand."

The rough skin of his thumb scrapes along my jaw before tipping my chin up to meet his somber gaze. He shakes his head, bending to rest his forehead against mine. "I want you to know everything about me, Antoinette. Just like I want to know everything about you. The good and the bad. I want you to know it all." A single tear cascades down his cheek, glittering in the fading sunlight. "We lost Roman four years ago, and it was the most painful thing I've been through besides losing my parents when I was in college. I've healed a lot over the past few years, but there are days I pick up the phone to call him and remember... I can't. It fucking hurts my heart." He clutches the fabric of his t-shirt where it rests over his heart. "But I still have Lily and Maggie, so I focus on them. Helping them fix up the house. Spending every birthday and holiday with them."

Sniffling, I brush away another tear from his cheek. "I can't imagine losing a sibling, let alone one you were so close to. I'm so sorry, Cyrus. Thank you for sharing your pain with me. I know I don't deserve it—"

His grip on my chin tightens until a zing of pain hits my nerve endings. "Why the fuck would you think you don't deserve it?" The command in his voice has me biting back a whimper that threatens to claw its way up my throat.

Peering up beneath my lashes, I whisper, "Because I hated you. Because I misjudged you."

In a hypnotic rhythm, his thumb strokes over my wind-blown cheek, warming the skin. "I thought we already straightened this mess out. I don't give a rat's ass that you hated me in the past. We both made mistakes. It's over and done, okay?"

I nod.

"You deserve to be here. You deserve to be touched and cared for and..." he trails off, eyes shutting when he clears his throat. *And what?*

When his eyes open again, they're burning fiercely, like the most extravagant sapphires. "Let's get one thing straight—I'm not in the habit of doing things I don't want. And I want you here, princess."

This time, when I shiver, it's not from the cold but from the possessiveness flaring in those beautiful eyes.

The gravel in his voice coats my skin, landing right between my thighs. How did we go from heartfelt and bone-deep to horny and feral in the blink of an eye?

Before I find the answer, his lips land on mine with a guttural groan that vibrates through my whole body.

I melt against him.

As his lips tangle with mine, my dragon roars to the surface and my skin heats.

Suddenly, my thin trench coat is too much and sweat beads down my back. I need to shift. I need to chase. I need to fuck him.

Now!

"Run," I order against his lips.

Wide-eyed, he breaks the kiss. "What?"

"Run. I need you to run for me, Cyrus. Will you be a good boy and let me chase you?"

It's second nature for a dragon to hunt its prey, but it's something I've never let myself indulge in.

Like I've been waiting for the *right* prey. And Cyrus Wilcox is the perfect little lamb to chase through the woods.

Tonight, under the rising autumn moon, I yearn to let my dragon have a little fun.

Stroking his face, I reassure him. "I won't hurt you. I promise. In fact, I think you'll rather enjoy being caught." I wink, the gesture full of filthy promise.

Full lips tilt into a wicked smile, and he backs away from me, hands raised. "Whatever you say, princess. Why don't you give me a head start?"

Then he disappears into the rows of apple trees.

Chapter 21

Cyrus

Moonlight streams through the leaves overhead, illuminating my path as my boots pound against the dirt. Sweat pours down the sides of my face, soaking the neckline of my shirt, and my breaths saw in and out of my chest.

When she said run, I thought she was joking.

I should have known better. The woman is serious about almost everything in her life. Why should this be any different?

Antoinette has awoken a side of me I never knew existed until the other night in our office. She's dominant and commanding, and I love every fucking minute of it. So if she wants to chase me through the woods and fuck me, then so be it.

I'm game.

Pumping my arms at my sides, my heart rampages in my chest, threatening to break free from its cage. My ears perk up, suddenly aware of every snapped twig and noise lurking in the darkness.

As I sprint, my cock thickens in my pants, the fear pumping through my veins morphing into arousal with each step I take.

Once I've made it a few hundred yards or so into the trees, I cut off the main path and press my back against a thick tree trunk. The wind whispers across my sweat-slicked skin, causing me to shiver.

Or maybe it's from the anticipation of Antoinette catching me and having her way with me.

Chest heaving, I slap a hand over my mouth to muffle the sound of my heavy breathing. Above the treetops, flames light up the sky, followed by an animalistic screech.

She's right there.

And I'm not ready for our chase to be over so soon. I tighten my muscles, remaining as still as possible until the beat of her wings fades into the distance and my heart rate slows to a light gallop. "Missed me, princess," I whisper before taking off deeper into the trees.

Far in the distance, the faint glow of light beckons me like a mirage in the desert.

The guest house.

If I can get inside the small cabin first, she'll be forced to shift back into human form, and I'll have the upper hand.

I'll be the predator instead of the prey.

My boots beat against the ground, crunching fallen leaves in my wake. On the other hand, I'm sure if she catches me, I'll enjoy whatever she does to me.

A whoosh of flapping wings rustles the leaves above me. I cut left and weave through the trees, trying to lose her.

But it's no use.

Golden eyes glint in the darkness, heading straight toward me. Her wings stir dust from the ground as she careens closer.

Fuck!

I can't let her catch me yet. I can't make it this easy.

Diving to the side, my shirt tears when I collide with the ground. Wet leaves and cold dirt scrape against the now exposed skin. Another angry screech hits my ears. When I peer over my shoulder, shimmering black scales cut through the trees, returning to the darkened sky.

By the skin of my teeth, I avoided capture.

However, now that she knows where I am, she'll be coming back any second, so I roll to my knees. Once I'm back on my feet, I strip off my sweat-soaked jacket and shirt. The autumn breeze against my damp skin sets a rush of goosebumps skittering across my flesh. I'm a sitting duck right here, so I fling the wet clothing into some nearby bushes, hoping to create a diversion.

Antoinette's vicious roar fills the blackened sky, and I take off in the opposite direction, toward the guest house at the far end of the property.

Blood rushes through my ears, and the harsh inhale and exhale of my breaths is the only thing I hear.

I must have lost her.

As the yellow glow of the guest house light comes into view, I slow my steps to a walk and spread my arms wide. Spinning in a circle, I taunt her. "Come on, princess! I know you can do better than that!" Lost to the darkness, my voice echoes away into the rows of apple trees, but I know better.

I know there's a predator lurking. Waiting. Biding her time.

To my right, a slight glint of gold catches my eye. *There she is.*

But before I can break into a run again, she leaps from the abyss, all sharp claws and vicious teeth shining in the moonlight.

She's fucking beautiful.

My back collides with the dirt, but it doesn't even hurt when she tackles me to the ground. I'm too fucking entranced by her dragon form. The opalescent sheen on her immaculately groomed black scales. The sheer membrane of her wings appears to be woven from the midnight sky itself, a myriad of constellations shimmering with each lazy movement.

Her spike-laden tail swishes behind her as she stalks over me, smoky breath fanning my face. Razor-sharp black claws dig into the earth on either side of my face when she leans in close. I can't tear my gaze from hers, the nictitating membrane the only sound in the dead of night.

Tilting her head to the side, she assesses me like any predator would its prey.

"What now, princess? You caught me."

Sweet smoke fills my nose when she huffs a breath, a low growl rumbling from her chest.

She's magnificent.

If I didn't know this was Antoinette, I'd be shitting my pants, but the familiar metallic gaze reassures me that I'm safe. This is my dragon to slay.

Not that I'm in a position to do any slaying.

At that moment, my cock jerks, pressing against the zipper of my jeans. Okay, maybe I do have a sword for this fight.

A familiar forked tongue slithers from behind sharp teeth. I shiver and moan when it makes contact with my overheated, clammy skin.

The rough texture drags up the center of my abs and over my left pec muscle, before the forks split and wrap around my nipple, tugging at the sensitive bud of flesh.

"God. *Yes.*" My voice is only a whisper, too focused on the pleasure she's giving me.

Thudding against the cool ground, I roll my head back and groan. No woman—no creature—has ever had this heady, animalistic effect on me. Like a rushing tidal wave, lust careens through my veins with each swipe of Antoinette's sinful tongue.

Thrusting my hips in the air, I seek any friction to relieve the ache in my cock. "Please, Antoinette."

Fuck, did I just beg? Who am I? What is this woman—this goddess—doing to me?

Heat licks the exposed skin on my chest and arms when the dragon prowling over me suddenly rears back, bursting into a dazzling display of crimson and orange flames.

Antoinette emerges from the fire a mere blink of my eyes later, but she's not quite fully human.

Shimmering black scales ripple along her cheekbones, down the sides of her neck to the tops of her heaving breasts. Along either side of her belly button, a strip of scales lines her soft abdomen, drawing my eyes downward, to the glistening slit between her spread thighs where she straddles my waist.

Long, black claw-like nails dig into my chest when she leans forward, bracing her weight on me. I wince against the pinpricks of pain, but my cock somehow hardens even more in my pants.

Not only do I crave being submissive to this woman, but apparently I'm a glutton for pain, too.

"You were such good prey, Cyrus." The purr of her voice has me panting. "Running like a scared little deer for me." Pointed white teeth glisten under the mellow glow of the full moon, giving her smile a menacing appearance, but somehow, she's still stunning. "Do you think you deserve a reward?"

Her raven hair flows to her shoulders in a wild mane. A dark crown fit for a dark queen.

My queen.

"Yes," I pant, hands gripping her hips and grinding her where I need it most... against my raging cock.

She tsks, wagging one claw-tipped finger in my face. "Nuh-ah. Naughty boy." My fingers sting when her hand connects with the flesh, and I grit my teeth.

I flash back to the night in our office and instantly know the words she wants to hear. "Yes, ma'am," I rasp.

"Good boy." That same menacing smile lights up her face, eyes liquified with lust.

Movement behind her draws my attention. For the first time, I notice wings flapping lazily at her back and a smooth tail swishing against my leg. They're the same as her full dragon form, only a smaller scale to fit her human body.

Before I can find my voice, she slinks down my body until her face is poised over the obvious bulge in my jeans. *Fuck, touch me. Please!*

My body trembles, and I clench my fists at my sides to resist the urge to rip open my pants and stroke myself. I get the feeling that would be disobeying her and would result in the end to our little game of cat and mouse. Something I surely don't want.

Fabric tears, and a cold gust of air against my legs snaps me back to the present.

"D-Did you just—?" I spring up to my elbows.

Antoinette smirks, tattered strips of denim and cotton clutched between her claws, a feral glint in her eyes.

At the sight, my hard cock weeps against my stomach, leaking a clear string of liquid. I think it's safe to say he's a big fan of being dominated.

"Fuuuuuck." When she finally wraps those long, delicate fingers around my shaft and gives a testing squeeze, I lose it, falling back onto the dirt. You'd think my dick's never been touched by a woman from the way my thigh muscles clench and the tip of my cock spills a river of pre-cum.

It's pathetic.

I'm embarrassed for myself.

"Such a good boy for me. Aren't you?" she coos, hand twisting as it works up and down my length, smearing the clear fluid until every inch of my hard cock glistens under the moonlight.

Blowing out a breath, I close my eyes and focus on my breathing so I don't blow my load too soon, but her hands on me are otherworldly. Soft, yet firm. Delicate, but forceful. Coaxing drop after drop of pleasure to fill my veins until I'm drowning in it.

It's the perfect mix of torture and it's driving me insane.

Determined fingers caress my balls, forcing a shuddering breath from my lungs. My hips buck as I chase the tight grip of her hand.

"Your mouth, princess. Give me your mouth." The words come out strained through gritted teeth.

I haven't had her mouth on me yet, and I know it will be... heaven.

I moan at the first swipe of that damn forked tongue. The one she's been teasing me with for weeks now. It's warm. Wet. And everything I want.

She suctions her lips around the tip of my cock and, I swear, my damn soul leaves my body, heart leaping in my chest. Groaning, my fingers dig into the dirt at my sides.

Silken black strands fall in front of her beautiful face, obscuring my view. We can't have that. I need her smoldering gaze on me while she sucks me dry.

Propping up on one elbow, I use my free hand to sweep the strands into my fist, revealing her golden eyes.

They lock with mine, heating me straight to my very core, as she sinks all the way down on my shaft until the tip of her elegant nose brushes the trimmed hairs on my pelvis.

I'm not a total caveman; I keep things groomed for my partners.

A shudder rolls through me when her throat muscles constrict, cheeks hollowing as she pulls back. "Damn, you're good at that." Somehow, I choke out the words.

"Come on, Wilcox," she chides, eyes dancing with humor while she hovers over my glistening cock, lips swollen and spit covered. "I'm a supernatural creature. Did you really think I'd have a gag reflex?"

But I don't get a chance to answer because she deepthroats me again, my fingers tightening in her hair.

She works my cock with her mouth and hands until I'm a quivering, moaning mess. I'm teetering on the edge of bliss when something blunt presses between my ass cheeks. "Wha—"

Popping off my cock, she places a single claw against my protesting lips. "Shhh, Wilcox. You're going to love this."

Her tail wraps around her torso, diving between her thighs. "Let me get it ready for you first." The tapered tip slips through her pussy lips, rubbing back and forth until it's coated in a sheen of her arousal.

"Do you trust me?" Her eyes glow with sincerity in the darkness.

I'll admit, I've always been curious about ass play and prostate stimulation. But I've never trusted anyone enough to try it. I've always been the dominant one in the bedroom. With Antoinette, I feel safe and free enough to explore my more submissive side. "Yes. I trust you, princess," I confirm with a nod.

Sufficiently lubricated, her tail slithers back between my legs, pressing under my balls to a place I've never explored before. I stiffen at the first hint of pressure against my tight pucker.

"Relax for me. I'd never hurt you, Cyrus. Tell me to stop if you don't want this."

I dive headfirst into the golden depths of her eyes and nod, swallowing past the lump in my throat, because something tells me I'm going to come harder than I ever have in my life. "Don't stop. I want everything you'll give me, princess."

"Good boy," she whispers in a husky voice. Her hand continues to fly up and down my spit-soaked shaft, ramping up my pleasure until I'm teetering on the edge of the cliff. Eyes locked on mine, the slick tip of her tail breaches the tight muscles of my ass.

A delicious burn radiates from the stretched hole as she slowly pushes further inside. "You okay?" Her eyebrows rise in question.

A choked "yeah" is all I can manage. Between the tight stroke of her hand on my cock and her tail rubbing against my prostate, I'm primed to explode.

Antoinette smirks, licking her lips with her eyes locked on my ass. "Your ass is so perfect, Cyrus. Wish you could see the way you stretch to take my tail." She shudders, eyes rolling into the back of her head.

"Does seeing your tail in my ass make you wet, princess?" I force the words out, hips snapping up to chase her hand before retreating in search of her tail. I'm caught in the middle of pleasure overload.

"You have no idea," she purrs. "I'm dripping for you."

Pumping into me a few times before curving, her tail hits a delicious spot that has my eyes rolling back. "So good. Keep going," I whimper, my skin heating at the first signs of my orgasm building at the base of my spine.

One more pump of her tail and it's like a sonic boom goes off in my body, rushing through me and releasing pleasure to every nerve ending. Locking eyes with her, I groan when the first rope of cum shoots from my cock onto my stomach.

Hand still gripped in her hair, I push her mouth back onto my spurting cock and moan. "Don't let it go to waste, princess."

She goes willingly, wrapping those pretty lips around my cock and swallowing me whole.

It's like the power dynamic between us has shifted in my favor. But my mind is too focused on my orgasm to care, so I hold her down and she gobbles up my release like a good girl while her tail pumps in and out of my ass.

Because I'm her good fucking boy.

CHAPTER 22

Antoinette

The salty tang of his cum coats my tongue as I sit back on my bare feet. My tail pulls free from Cyrus and coils behind me on the cool ground, causing a shiver to rush up my spine. His big chest heaves up and down as he gasps for breath, and his fists flex in the dirt at his sides. But there's a sly smile on his lips, dark lashes fluttering against his high cheekbones. "Damn, princess." He raises his head and I'm met by glacial-blue eyes that seem to glow in the moonlight. They're beautiful and hypnotic, just like him. "I don't think I've ever come that hard in my life."

Licking my lips, I smirk. "Told you. Aren't you glad you trusted me?"

His smile widens to match my own, and he sits up, reaching for me. "Mmm, so glad."

Pulling me into his lap, my tail has a mind of its own, curling around his back and holding him close.

Our noses brush, the ice in his eyes melting into a raging inferno of sapphire flames. "But it's my turn now. You're done running the show, princess."

My brow furrows. He just came; surely he can't be ready for round two already?

Glancing down, I raise an eyebrow. His dick lies flaccid atop his balls. I'll admit, it's still impressive in size even though it's not hard. Tingles erupt between my thighs. "How do you expect to fuck me with a limp dick?"

A dark chuckle rings through the midnight air. "You're going to sit on my face until I'm ready to fuck you."

My mouth falls open before I can catch myself. I'm not easy to shock, but Cyrus Wilcox keeps finding new ways to throw me off my game. Why? How?

One finger tucks under my chin, effectively closing my mouth as his graveled voice coats my skin. "Now, turn around and get that perfect pussy and ass on my mouth. I'm starving, princess."

An unexpected whimper crawls up my throat, and I shiver, body moving of its own free will.

Obeying his filthy command, I turn around when Cyrus lies back on the ground. As I back up and straddle his face, his big hands warm my already heated skin and my nipples stiffen to painful peaks. Moaning, I twist them between my claws, settling my dripping core right over his waiting mouth.

"That's it, Antoinette." He tugs me closer, to the point his breaths heat my pussy. "Show me you can be my good girl, just as much as I can be your good boy."

I'm not usually a fan of cunnilingus, but Cyrus has shown in the past to know what he's doing. The man is a vigorous eater and, last time, I came so fucking hard. I'm willing to let him try again.

"You weren't lying, were you?" His finger runs through my pussy. "You really are dripping."

Before I can respond, a wet heat prods at my opening. The first swipe of his tongue is my undoing. My body convulses and I lose all ability to speak or think; I'm simply a conduit for pleasure. All I can do is moan and rock my hips against his mouth.

Cyrus groans, his fingers digging into the extra fat on my hips and pulling me closer, like he can't get enough. His tongue invades my cunt, the ribbed channel rippling to make way as he fucks me with his mouth.

My wings unfurl, rustling my hair where the sweaty strands stick to my shoulders and cheeks. "Cyrus, please," I whine. Head tipping down, my gaze is transfixed on his jaw as it works to bring me to orgasm. *I'm so close.*

He stops.

Lifting me a mere centimeter from his lips, his voice is muffled. "Use your words, princess. Tell me what you need."

Oh! The fucking nerve!

I scoff. Reaching back, I card my claws through his silken hair. Gripping tight, I pull until he grunts. "Listen here, Wilcox—"

A crack sounds through the silence. A moment later, a sharp sting on my ass resonates. I yelp, but it quickly turns into a moan.

"Did you just spank me?"

Another crack, another zip of pain in my ass cheek.

He growls, my fingers still buried in his hair, no doubt suffocating him against my cunt and ass. "Use." *Slap.* "Your." *Slap.* "Words." *Slap.*

A gush of wetness leaks from my cunt, and I tip my head back with another moan. I get off on a little pain. He's probably figured that out by now.

My body vibrates with the need to orgasm, so I give in to the asshole beneath me. "Please, Cyrus. Put that smart mouth to good use and make me come my damn brains out!" I scream into the midnight sky.

His answering dark chuckle only adds to the quivering in my body. "As you wish, princess."

Then his tongue is back where it belongs—inside me, buried deep, and stroking that perfect spot.

My claw-tipped fingers find their way to my clit, and I rub like my life depends on it. Sparks of pleasure ripple under my skin, sending me racing toward my orgasm. "Right there, Cyrus."

An open palm lands on the fleshy mound of my ass one last time, the sting radiating through my body and rocketing me to my peak.

I throw my head back, pleasure bowing my spine and the tips of my outstretched wings brushing the soil as shock waves overtake me. "Cyrus!" My shattered cry rips from my lungs, floating up to the full moon.

Finally spent, I tip forward, one hand wrapping around Cyrus's throat. The thick muscles contract when he swallows down my sweet nectar, moaning like he can't possibly get enough. "That's it, my sweet prey. Such a good boy."

He groans, and the vibrations on my oversensitive clit have me moaning. A little pain never hurt anyone.

My wings and tail retract now that the burning lust and urge to chase have drained from my body. Standing on shaky legs, I turn and extend a hand to Cyrus. "Come on, Wilcox. You're filthy. Let's go take a shower. And I believe you promised me round two."

S team fogs the glass of the small shower stall as Cyrus pounds into me. His grip is bruising on my thighs, where he holds me against the smooth tiled wall. "Fuck, princess," he moans against my neck. "I don't think I'll ever get over how amazing your pussy feels. Not for as long as I live."

My claws scrape against his back muscles, but I make sure not to break the skin. The lump in my throat grows, and I swallow, attempting to push it down, but it's no use.

What we did earlier—him letting me chase him and have my way with him in the woods—I've never done that with anyone before. Never trusted anyone enough to show them my true desires.

Cyrus is different.

The connection between us is deeper.

And it scares me more than being forced to leave home at eighteen or being the only woman in a boardroom full of men.

He could hurt me.

He could shatter the organ in my chest that's finally come back to life.

"Antoinette." He moans my name like a prayer, and that's when the first tear falls. I want him, but I'm afraid of what that means, so I focus on the here and now.

I focus on the rhythm of his hips. The stretch of his cock. The hot breath against my neck.

I focus on the pleasure he's filling my body with. The inevitable orgasm I know he'll give me.

We can figure out the messy feelings later.

Face buried against my flesh, his teeth sink into my neck, and I scream, my cunt tightening around his cock. My own teeth lengthen to sharp points, aching with the need to slice open his flesh and transfer my immortality to him.

But I can't.

Not yet anyway.

We haven't talked about the future.

Would he even want to live forever?

Does he want to be shackled to a selfish, closed-off workaholic like me for eternity?

A prick of pain when he releases my skin pulls me back to the present. His hips piston, cock hitting that spot deep inside, and pushing me toward orgasm.

His hand fists in the back of my hair, lips pressed against my skin as I find my release at the same time he does.

"Antoinette," Cyrus groans. "Take all of me. It's yours. I'm yours. I—" His words cut off on a pained moan, hips stuttering to a stop when my cunt locks around him as I come.

My heart beats wildly in my chest. The pleasure fades from my veins and a single tear rolls down my cheek. Wrapping my arms around Cyrus's neck, I cling to him while the shower water beats down on us.

I love Cyrus Wilcox.

The sudden realization hits me like a ton of bricks. It's heart stopping. Soul shattering. All-consuming.

And it scares the ever-loving shit out of me how much I want to keep him.

CHAPTER 23

Antoinette

The guest house is more of a tiny cabin sitting at the back of Maggie's property. It's one open space with high ceilings and large windows, making it seem larger than it really is.

A small kitchen area is tucked near the front door. Miniature appliances line the walls, and there's just enough butcher-block counter space for food preparation. Extending from the wall, a peninsula houses two barstools and divides the kitchen from the living room.

The living room consists of a couch and chair nestled in front of a brick fireplace. Flames currently dance in the hearth while Cyrus and I lie in the queen-sized bed shoved into the back corner of the cabin.

A small, but newly remodeled, bathroom is located on the other side of the front door from the kitchen.

It's homey and quaint.

The perfect escape from the noise and chaos of city life.

A gentle breeze from the open window above the bed ruffles my damp hair where it fans across the pillow. Turning my head, moonbeams spill through the open curtains, casting Cyrus in a soft glow.

Dark-blonde strands of hair fall over his forehead, his eyebrows scrunched until a deep V forms between them.

I run a finger along his jaw; my nails are back to their normal almond shape. The only remnants of my inner dragon are my usual golden eyes and a few scales peeking through my skin.

My finger makes its way up to his forehead, sweeping the fallen hairs back to reveal his strong but furrowed brow.

When I smooth my finger between them, his eyebrows relax as I ask, "What is it?"

He's been quiet since our shower, which is unusual for him. Although, I've been a little trapped in my own head, too, processing my emotions. Maybe he's doing the same. Tonight was a big step for us. Meeting his family. Opening up about his brother.

Not to mention our fuckfest among the trees. All of which I'm grateful for.

The muscle in his jaw flexes before he turns his head, the pillow scrunching beneath his weight. "Why do you think O'Malley won't sign the contract?"

I sigh. This is something that has been heavy on my mind, too. The old man is stubborn, that's for sure. "Honestly, I'm not sure. The offer is very generous, more than what the place is worth. And he seemed genuinely happy at every meeting. But ..."

My words trail off, gaze falling as I tuck the comforter tighter around my naked body, suddenly aware of how exposed and vulnerable I am.

I'm not used to this.

Discussing my feelings with someone else. Letting someone in.

A finger hooks underneath my chin, tipping it up until I'm met by crystal clear icy eyes. "Tell me, Antoinette. I'm on your side."

My throat clicks with a swallow before I speak. "If he doesn't sign that contract, I'm fucked. You heard Andrews—he won't hesitate to fire me, even though I'm his top agent."

"Fuck Andrews," Cyrus responds immediately.

A bitter, forced laugh bursts from my mouth.

Propping onto his elbow, he rests a hand on the small of my waist. His warmth seeps through the thin fabric of the patchwork quilt, and I take comfort in the weight of his touch on my tired body. Eyes locked with mine, he says, "I know you can handle this situation on your own, and I'm not doubting you. We're a team, remember?"

I nod.

"So, do you want me to call O'Malley next week and see if I can convince him to sign the contract?"

My dragon bristles, fury sparking low in my veins. Smoke stings the tiny hairs at the back of my nostrils. Old habits die hard.

Slamming my eyes shut, I hold my breath and conjure up an image of eyes reminiscent of an arctic glacier. Serene. Calm. Chilling.

Instantly, the fire in my veins extinguishes.

Like fucking magic.

My eyes spring open.

Cyrus is my magic.

"Yes," I finally answer. "I would really appreciate your help."

Soft lips land on my forehead, and I sigh as he murmurs, "Always, princess."

I'm in so deep with this man. I can only hope and pray he doesn't shatter my heart before we're done. But I don't want to think about the inevitable moment of our demise right now. I'd much rather enjoy the last few moments of relaxation in our cozy bubble in the woods.

So I do.

Pushing Cyrus to his back, I nestle under his arm and snuggle against his chest. The steady thumping of his heart fills my ear when I melt into his side.

Strong fingers stroke through my damp hair and down my back as they wander under the quilt. He squeezes my ass cheek before starting back again at my hair. Over and over, he caresses me and everything else fades away.

My own fingers weave a path through the smattering of hair on his chest. It's the perfect amount; enough so you know he's not some young cub, but not too much that he looks like a bear.

"Have you ever thought about moving out here? To help Maggie?" I ask, eyes drooping.

"Nah." He chuckles. "My life is in the city, going toe to toe with a feisty dragon shifter to find the next hit property before anyone else."

I roll my eyes even though he can't see. But a smile pulls at the corner of my lips, knowing he wants to be in the city—to be near *me*.

Still stroking my back, he goes on. "In all seriousness, Maggie would hate having me here. She's strong... and stubborn. She's an amazing mom, and I'd only be in the way, so I come out almost every Sunday to take care of anything she needs help with, and I pay for what little she'll let me. I know Roman had a life insurance policy, so I assume she and Lily are financially okay."

My heart breaks for Maggie. There were pictures all over the main house of her and Roman. It's clear she did, and still does, love him very much. I can't imagine losing your soulmate. My arm tightens around Cyrus, holding him as close to me as possible. "I was wrong about you, Cyrus. Your heart is so big. I can't imagine losing the people closest to you but finding the strength to keep going."

He shrugs, jostling my body. "It hasn't been easy. If anything, it's made me and Maggie closer. But she can't do it on her own forever. I actually hired a nanny for her this summer. Hopefully, she isn't too pissed when she finds out. I just want her to have some time for herself so she can unwind and relax a little."

"Well, out here, away from the hustle and bustle of city life, seems like the perfect place to relax. You were right. I needed a weekend away... and no more work on weekends," I say with a nod of committal.

I'm supposed to be a predator, but somehow, Cyrus moves quick as lightning, caging me beneath him. My eyes spring wide, hands gripping his taut biceps.

"I'm sorry; can you say that again?" A devilish smirk plays on his lips.

Eyebrows scrunching, it takes me a second to figure out what in the hell he's talking about. "You were ri—" Mid-sentence, it hits me... so I hit *him*, both hands slapping against his firm chest muscles, knocking him back with an *oomph*.

"Asshole! You had to ruin our perfectly good pillow-talk, didn't you?"

That damn smirk is fixed firmly on his lips and, I'll be honest, it's grown on me. This once insufferable man has chipped away at my castle walls every day for the past month.

Leaning down, his mouth lands on mine, and I forget what we were talking about altogether when his tongue slides between my lips. Moaning, I wrap my legs around his waist and pull him closer, needing more of his taste on my tongue.

Breaking the kiss, he rests his forehead against mine, face serious as he whispers, "I'm sorry, princess. You're just so fun to rile up."

Before I can land another playful smack on his chest, he rolls to his back again, tucking me into his side.

"Thank you for indulging my fantasy earlier."

He chuckles. "You mean letting you chase me through the trees? That was your fantasy?"

I smile. Propping onto my elbow, I meet his sleepy gaze. "One of them. We can get to the rest another day. It means a lot to me that you put your trust in my hands, Cyrus."

"I know you'd never hurt me, princess."

My chest warms at his words. At the trust growing between us. I've never had this with anyone else. "D-do you have any fantasies you want to try?"

When my eyes skate down to his crotch, the sheet is slightly tented. Interesting. Something's got him turned on.

He clears his throat, drawing my gaze back to his face. "I've never admitted this to anyone." His chest heaves under me when he blows out a breath. "But I've always wanted to have a partner give me total control. To fill her sweet pussy whenever I want."

My blood heats with arousal. Could I give him that? Freedom to use me whenever he wants?

"Like when I'm asleep?" It's something I've secretly wanted to try, but never trusted anyone enough to admit.

"Yeah."

"Okay." I stroke a hand up his chest to rest over his heart. It's thudding like crazy. "I trust you, Cyrus. We can try that whenever you're ready."

He smiles, pulling me in for one more kiss before I snuggle against his side, tucking the blanket around us.

This feels right.

Like where I'm meant to spend my nights after long days in the office.

Yawning, I push the scary thoughts of the future out of my mind and murmur, "Goodnight, Cyrus."

Suddenly, the day's events catch up to me—meeting his family, the chase through the orchard, and our subsequent fuckfest—and weariness sweeps through me, so I wriggle closer to Cyrus and let the thumping of his heart lull me to the edge of sleep. The last words to greet my ears before I tumble to dreamland are "Goodnight, princess."

CHAPTER 24

Cyrus

The line trills in my ear as the call room door clicks
shut behind me. Cellphone clutched to my ear, I
pace the small space while I wait for Mr. O'Malley to pick
up.

After our weekend away, Antoinette and I spent this
week putting the final touches on the warehouse presentation.

The only piece missing is the old man's signature. I've
been procrastinating on this call because my gut tells me
there's a reason he hasn't signed the contract yet.

Each floor of the building has a few closet-sized rooms designated for private calls. This particular room overlooks the river, and a tour boat passing in the distance catches my attention while my phone continues to ring.

"Aye."

Finally! "Mr. O'Malley?"

"Aye."

Man of few words.

Clearing my throat, I continue pacing. "Good morning, sir. This is Cyrus Wilcox. I'm calling from Big York on behalf of Antoinette Bauer. Do you have a moment to chat?"

There's a shuffling of papers, then a cough. "Aye, the dragon shifter." He chuckles. "Real temper on that one."

My eyebrows wing upward. "How did you—"

"I wasn't born yesterday, laddie. I knew the lass had a dragon in her the second I laid eyes on her. Some supernaturals may be able to hide in plain sight, but you can't hide from magic."

"Magic?" I scratch the back of my head. This conversation is taking an unexpected turn.

"Ya see, us O'Malleys come from a long line of psychics, seers, and the like."

"Is that why you haven't signed the contract yet? Because Antoinette isn't human? If that's the case, you can shove—"

"Aye! You've got it all wrong, sonny. This warehouse is meant to be *hers*, not *theirs*."

Well, if that's not cryptic as fuck. "What the fu—heck does that mean?" I growl, trying to tamp down the anger in my veins because he's still a client, and we still need his signature.

The whole project is riding on one measly signature. All of Antoinette's brilliant ideas won't mean anything without it.

If we lose this property, we're both fucked.

If Andrews fires both of us, it'll hurt for a second, but at least we'll still have each other.

If he only fires Antoinette, there's no way she'll want to be with me.

My heart ricochets against my ribs at the thought of her rejecting me. I'm in too deep now; I love her.

"Sir, you have to sign those papers. This property is Antoinette's biggest deal to date. All that's standing in her way is your signature."

"Don't worry your pretty head, Mr. Wilcox. It will be hers when the time is right. Things always have a way of workin' out. And laddie..."

"Hmm?" My ears perk up. Maybe he's changed his mind.

"You best take care of that woman. Treat her like the princess she is. She deserves nothing but the best."

Of that, I'm certain he's one thousand percent correct.

With his cryptic message ringing in my ear, the line goes dead. The old man hung up on me.

"Fuck!" My voice echoes around the small room, and my phone thunks to the floor. Both hands thread through my hair, pulling at the strands until a rush of pain zips down my spine. "What am I gonna tell Antoinette?"

She's already on edge from Andrews's earlier threat. A perpetual cloud of smoke wafts behind her with the amount of stress she's under to make this presentation perfect.

I don't want to lie to her, but this could be the last straw before she breaks. She can't take any bad news right now.

Sweat beads on my forehead, and I swallow back the bile crawling up my throat as I exit the call room and head back to my office. One way or another, this situation isn't going to end well for me. I can already tell.

I just hope it doesn't mean losing the woman I love.

Slowing my steps, I linger outside the office doorway, eavesdropping on Antoinette and Penelope while I calm my racing nerves.

"Annie, you have to breathe." Penelope coughs. I'm sure she's following Antoinette around the office with the red fire extinguisher clutched to her chest. "Everything will be fine. You and Cyrus have worked day in and day out on this presentation. You're ready."

Yeah, except we don't have a signed contract with the property owner.

"What if they hate it? I was stupid to think this would work. I'm suggesting Big York take on an entirely new business venture. It'll never work. They're going to fire me." Her voice doesn't hold its usual confidence or fire, and my gut drops to the floor.

Bursting through the doorway, I lock eyes with Antoinette. "I don't want to hear any more talk like that, princess." Stepping in front of her, I grip her slender shoulders and pull her into my chest.

She melts against me, the familiar heat of her body washing away my earlier jitters.

"Your concept is amazing, Antoinette. If the board can't see that, then it's their loss. We can both quit and find some investors who will back your idea. Just say the word, and I'll follow you out those doors." I tip my chin toward the glass doors of our office.

Her head swivels back and forth, the soft strands of ebony gliding against my shirt.

Arching her neck, she meets my eyes as she speaks. "You're right." The fire returns to her brilliant golden irises, like glittering gemstones. "I've given this project everything I have." She blows out a breath, fresh resolve cementing over her beautiful features. "I'm ready for tomorrow. I'm ready to knock them dead."

"That's my girl." I smile, cupping her cheek.

"How did it go with O'Malley?" Expectantly, her eyebrows rise.

Before leaving for the privacy of the call room, I'd told both Antoinette and Pen that I was going to make the dreaded call to O'Malley.

Shit. It's one tiny lie, Cyrus. It'll be fine. O'Malley said the warehouse would be hers, so what's the harm in protecting her for now?

The harm is that she finally trusts me, and this teeny tiny lie could ruin everything.

Rolling my shoulders back, I blow out a breath and slide my hands down to the sides of her neck. My thumb rests over her pulse, giving me the boost I need to tell her the truth. "Not as well as I'd hoped."

Under my hands, her skin heats to a scorching temperature, and I nearly pull away. But she needs support and reassurance right now. She needs to know she's not alone in this. "He hasn't signed the papers—but he did promise the warehouse would be yours."

Eyes shuttering, she pulls from my grip and paces the small space between me and her desk. "No, no, no, no. This can't be happening." A plume of smoke trails behind her, and I wave my hand, clearing it from the air.

Maybe lying would have been easier. *No. Suck it up, Cyrus. You can't build a relationship on lies.*

"Princess."

Her heels click on the tile as she paces. I've seen her spiral like this once before, but this time is different. This time, I can be the comfort she needs.

"Princess." My arm shoots out, stopping her path.

Gripping her chin between my forefinger and thumb, I swing her head toward me. With my free hand, I point at my eyes. "Look at me, Antoinette."

She scowls, eyes blazing, but meets my gaze. An invisible presence ruffles the dark strands of hair as they hang around her shoulders. Black scales rip through the flesh of her cheeks and down her neck, dipping into the neckline of her blouse. She's close to losing control, and I can't let that happen.

Ignoring the lingering burn on my palms, I cup her scorching hot cheeks and dip closer. "This isn't all on you. Okay? I'm in this with you until the end. No matter what happens. We're partners on this project, so you focus on knocking this presentation out of the park, and I'll deal with O'Malley. Yeah?"

She nods, her skin cools slightly, and the smoke between us dissipates.

"Now, what else can I do to help?"

"I don't like waiting on O'Malley, but there's nothing we can do this close to the presentation. Will you help me run through everything one more time?" Her fingers thread through mine. The sun streams in from the windows behind us, casting her in an ethereal glow. Her hair brushes her shoulders when she tips her head back, waiting for my reply.

"Of course. Lead the way."

"Thank you for staying with me tonight." Antoinette stands in the doorway of her en-suite bathroom, dressed in a short, silky nightgown. Her hand glides up and down one arm, rubbing lotion into her olive-toned skin. Subtle notes of lavender waft to where I'm settled in her bed.

We spent the rest of the day running through the warehouse presentation over and over until she was satisfied. Once the sky began to darken with the first signs of sunset, I convinced her to spend the evening relaxing with some mindless TV and pizza.

Now, I want nothing more than to curl around her while she sleeps.

Tucking an arm behind my head, I sink into the pillows. "Not like it's a hardship, princess. Your bed is a million times more comfortable than mine." I sigh. "Like sleeping on a cloud."

Her throaty laughter has me smirking. I love that sound.

Over the last week, her laughter has become more frequent. Is it because of me?

I'd like to think so.

I'd like to think Antoinette is freer now, more relaxed around me, and able to show all facets of her amazing personality.

She disappears into the bathroom, returning a few seconds later, and flips off the light before heading toward the bed. Sinking onto the mattress next to me, she lets out a groan that goes straight to my dick. "This bed *is* amazing. So much better than yours."

I scoff. We've only spent one night at my place, and Antoinette was restless the entire time. Tossing and turning, like the mattress was made out of bricks.

It's obvious she's more comfortable in the nest she's created here than my boring bachelor pad, so I don't mind spending all my free time here, in her sanctuary. "Guess you'll have to clear out some closet space for me, then."

Flipping to her side, she searches my face, a crease forming between her eyebrows. Shit, I guess it's too soon to bring up the topic of moving in together.

"You'd want to move in here? With me?"

I bite my tongue to stop the laugh from spilling free. But she looks so damn cute, flushed cheeks, lip caught between her fang, and hope-filled eyes.

"Yeah, princess. I told you before, but I'll remind you again—you're it for me, Antoinette Bauer." My thumb sweeps across her lower lip, dislodging it from her biting grip. "And your place is *way* cooler than mine." I wink.

A beaming smile sweeps across her face. "I have an extra key, and you can bring some things over tomorrow after the presentation..."

At the word presentation, her expression falls, morphing into one of dread. I've never seen her like this. She's always so confident and sure of herself. My hand brushes to the side of her neck, thumb stroking over her racing pulse. "You're nervous."

She nods.

"Come here." When I open my arms for her, she crawls over immediately and snuggles against my side. She's so warm, and her sweet floral aroma calms my runaway emotions, grounding me to her. My fingers thread into her hair, massaging her scalp until she melts against me. "You're ready, Antoinette. This project is your baby, and no one knows it like you do. Not even me. You know every little detail and all the ways to make it shine. You're going to blow them away tomorrow, and I'll be right there by your side." After I wring O'Malley's neck for waiting until the last minute to sign the damn contract.

"You're right." Her lips brush against my skin, like the soft caress of butterfly wings, pulling me out of my spiraling thoughts.

"Of course I am. You're Antoinette Bauer. You don't take 'no' for an answer."

She peers up at me, lips stretched in a weak smile. "Thank you for reminding me, Wilcox. I'm gonna make that presentation my bitch."

Hauling her up my body, I seal my lips to hers. When I pull back, I murmur, "Damn straight, princess. Show 'em who's boss."

Before I can take her tantalizing lips in another kiss, she covers her mouth and yawns.

As much as I want to take things further, I know she needs a good night's sleep before tomorrow, so my dick will have to wait. Once she's tucked against my side again, I pull the blanket up around us and press my lips to the crown of her head. "You're gonna do great." A yawn slips from my mouth. "Sweet dreams, princess."

Her answering soft snores lull me to sleep.

Chapter 25

Antoinette

H ot breath fans across my cheek, pulling a moan from my throat. I'm hovering on the edge of sleep and wakefulness. A fluffy haze fills my body as pressure ebbs between my thighs, and a warm weight lingers above me.

Responding to the subtle rocking of my body, my eyelids flutter, trying—and failing—to pull me from my slumber. The last thing I remember is falling asleep sprawled across—

"Shhh, princess. You don't have to wake up, but I need you to lock that sweet pussy around my cock. Can you do that for me?" Cyrus's rich voice echoes through my dreams, and I sink further into the pleasure surging in my veins. It radiates from my stretched pussy to the tips of my fingers.

"Yes, Cyrus. Don't stop." My voice is a soft rasp, still clinging to the last remnants of sleep.

My sleep-addled brain finally catches up. Days after our conversation at the guest house, Cyrus is following through with his fantasy. The thought of him being so needy that he had to slide into my pussy while we were sleeping has me on the brink of orgasm.

With slow, measured thrusts, he rolls his hips at just the right angle so his cock drags against my G-spot every time.

Tingles erupt through my sleepy body.

One thumb rests against my clit, creating the perfect amount of pressure to have me floating into a cloud of bliss. And like he coaxed, my inner walls seize up around his length, where it's buried deep inside me.

"Oh, fuck." His words are a low grunt spilled against my ear. "Yes, baby, your cunt is strangling me. I'm gonna reward you with my cum now, princess. Do you want that? To be leaking my cum when you wake up in the morning?"

My eyelids flutter again, this time opening to find Cyrus's unruly blonde hair tickling my nose while he nuzzles against my neck. "Yes, Cyrus. Give me everything."

He pulls back, half-lidded gaze filled with sleep and lust as his hips rock in a gentle rhythm, like ocean waves lap-ping at the shore. "Go back to sleep, princess. I'm almost there."

I shake my head, wrapping my arms around his broad back. "I'm awake now. Make me come again."

By now, my pussy has released its death grip on his cock, and I'm ready for another trip above the clouds.

Orgasming is a similar serotonin boost to flying. Both experiences make me weightless, like I'm floating outside my body. It's addicting, and right now, I need more of it from him.

Suddenly, sleep-rumpled Cyrus is gone. In his place, the dominant alpha from the corporate world springs into action, rolling to his back so I'm left straddling his muscular thighs and slim waist. His cock never leaves my channel as we switch to the new position.

If anything, he sinks deeper, hitting that perfect spot only he can reach.

Eyes locked on mine, he strokes his fingers over my cheekbone, whispering, "Show me how you ride a cock, my beautiful dragon queen."

The soft words ring with sincerity. My walls crumble, and my dragon surges from my chest. Hot to the touch, my skin warms as his fingers trail over the now visible shimmering black scales.

Following the sweep of his fingertips across my cheek and down to my lips, his eyes fill with so much adoration.

It takes everything in me not to spill the three little words that have been circling my brain—and my
heart—for the past week.

I love you.

Instead, I lean down and capture his mouth with mine.
Searing lips crash together like turbulent ocean waves as
I rock my hips, gliding my soaked core up and down his
length.

Breaking the kiss, he clasps his hands around my hips,
guiding me to ride him faster.

Head tipped back against the pillows, he groans. "You're
going to ruin me for anyone else, aren't you?"

Bracing my palms on his chest, his words push me over
the edge, and my dragon bursts from my skin. My wings
unfurl behind me. Claws lengthen to scrape against his
flesh, making him moan. "It's only fair, Cyrus. You've
already ruined me." One claw-tipped hand slips around his
throat as I make my confession.

Cyrus's hands slide up my sides until they're cupping
my breasts. The flesh tingles in his hold, nipples peaked
and ready to play. "That's it, princess. Let her out for me."
His eyes nearly burn my skin when they linger on the scales
running between my breasts and down my stomach.

Clearly, he likes what he sees.

With the little confidence boost, I straighten, hair ruffling when my wings extend to their full span. My tail
wraps around Cyrus's leg, and my hips continue to roll

against him, taking us higher and higher as we careen toward euphoria.

"Fuck, you're so beautiful." His blue eyes blaze in the dark, scorching every exposed inch of skin and scales. "Damn. Look at you. Riding cock like it's your job."

I choke a laugh, and he groans as my cunt spasms around his length. "Shut up, Cyrus. Or I'll have to gag you." Tightening my fingers around his neck until my claws break the skin, I let him know how serious my words are.

A dark chuckle vibrates from his throat. "Don't threaten me with a good time, princess."

I roll my eyes, but hips never stopping, I tip my head back and focus on the pleasure building in my core. I'm almost there.

"Fuck, you feel good," Cyrus groans. "Do that thing with your tail again—please."

My head snaps up until my eyes meet his. They're oozing with desperation, teeth digging into his bottom lip.

I know what he wants, but I'm not above a little teasing right now.

Uncoiling my tail from his leg, it flicks through the air behind me. Taunting him. "What thing?"

Big hands clutch my hips, and he moans. Thrusting up from beneath me, Cyrus fills my slick cunt over and over again with each piston of his hips. I shiver when the tip of his cock hits the perfect spot, and my eyes roll back into my head.

"You're gonna make me say it, aren't you? Devious woman." His words are clipped and hoarse, hips snapping up to meet each roll of my own.

My hand is still around his throat, the muscles bobbing when he swallows.

"Be a good boy and tell me what you want, Wilcox." I want him to *beg*. Something about knowing I'm what he needs to get off right now has me... *giddy*.

And I don't do giddy.

"Goddamnit." He groans again. "Put your tail in my ass, princess. I've never come as hard as I did that night in the woods. I need it again."

...And there it is.

A wolfish smile splits my lips. "Good boy," I moan as he grinds my clit along his pubic bone. I'm teetering on the edge of orgasm, but I need him to come with me.

Bringing the tip of my tail to his mouth, I raise an eyebrow. "Get it nice and wet first."

His eyes widen, but his mouth falls open.

He really is such a good boy.

Fisting the smooth scales, his tongue peeks out and trails over the sensitive underside. A shiver rushes through me at the first swipe of his tongue. So wet and warm.

Reaching the tapered tip, he sucks my tail into his mouth. I groan and rock my hips. The ribbed walls of my cunt flutter around his hard length.

My dragon's instincts take over, and I shove my tail deeper into his hot mouth until I hit the back of his throat. Cyrus gags, tears welling in his eyes.

But he doesn't stop.

He's not a quitter.

No, quite the opposite.

Sucking in air through his nose, Cyrus bobs his head, working my tail like it's a cock. I'm entranced by the way he slurps it in and out of his mouth until it's glistening with his spit.

"Damn, that's hot, Wilcox," I groan, unable to peel my eyes away from where the black scales shimmer under the moonlight with each bob of his head.

He groans, and the vibrations ripple from the tip of my tail right to my oversensitive clit.

My pussy clenches when Cyrus's throat muscles contract around my sensitive tail. I've never experienced anything more erotic in my life.

The way Cyrus didn't question it when I pushed past his lips, it's like he was made for me. *Damn.* "You're such a good boy."

Those simple words of praise pull another moan from his mouth and have goosebumps lifting across his flesh.

With one final push to the back of his throat, I relish the slight gag he makes before I pull my tail free. It's coated in his saliva. Slick and glistening. Ready for his ass.

His thrusts stop as my tail slithers behind us, disappearing from sight. Slowly, I press between his ass cheeks, searching for his tight pucker.

A guttural groan fills the air, and his fingers pinch into the fat of my hips when I breach the tight ring of muscle.

"Relax for me," I coo, tail pressing forward slowly, giving him enough time to change his mind.

But he doesn't. Grip tightening on my hips, he moans. "Don't stop. Fuck, please."

His lashes glisten with moisture. I press deeper and curl the tip of my tail against his prostate, pulling a feral groan from his heaving chest. "Yes, princess. Right there."

Seeing this arrogant man brought to literal tears of pleasure fills me with a whole new level of confidence. He's so willing to let me fuck him in half-dragon form. He didn't question my need to chase and dominate him the other night in the woods.

Not only can we go toe to toe in the corporate world, but we can go toe to toe in the bedroom, too. I've finally found my true sexual equal in Cyrus. Because as much as I need to be in charge, I secretly love when he takes control of my body and tells me what to do, too.

A sudden sharp pain in my nipple rips me from my thoughts. "Stay with me, Antoinette, because I'm not gonna last much longer."

Skilled fingers pluck and roll my nipples, adding another layer of pleasure as my hips pick up pace. "I'm right here.

Now come for me, Wilcox. Fill my cunt with your seed and claim what's yours." Leaning my hands on his chest, I grind down hard at the same time my tail curves inside his ass.

Cyrus's back arches off the bed. His broken groan is joined by my own pleasured moans when the first pulse of his release hits my core. My inner muscles lock, suffocating his cock. Claws digging into his chest, I freefall into my orgasm with my eyes locked on his beautiful blue ones.

This is what I want for the rest of my life. I know that now.

Once the orgasm fades, my gaze falls to his chest. It's marred by red lines, oozing with crimson blood. I should probably be riddled with guilt for hurting him.

Instead, pride flares in my chest.

These marks are a claiming.

He's mine.

Leaning down, I drag the forks of my tongue through the coppery liquid where it trickles from the open wounds. The salty tang coats my tongue, causing my teeth to ache. That familiar need to bite him takes over, and my vision flickers.

Totally unaware of my inner turmoil, Cyrus grabs my face and slams his lips to my bloodied ones. "That was like nothing I've ever experienced, Antoinette. You've definitely ruined me for anyone else."

His sweet kisses calm the dragon raging under my flesh, and I push down the need to sink my teeth into his neck... for a little while longer, anyway.

"You know," I say, leaning my forehead against his. A puff of warm air hits my lips as he groans when my tail slips free of his ass. "You letting me fuck your tight ass is probably one of the hottest things I've ever experienced."

Blunt teeth nip at my bottom lip, his tongue licking a soothing path right after. "Yeah?"

After a final peck to his lips, I roll to the side, settling against the pillows so I can see him. Dark-blonde hair is messy from my hands. His muscled chest, arms, and abs glisten with a fine layer of sweat.

Wet with our combined releases, his thick cock lays against his stomach. Damn, he's impressive even after I drained him dry.

But my eyes linger the longest on the bloodied scratch marks on his broad chest. "I've never had sex half-shifted with anyone else." My eyes flick to his, intense and un-blinking. "I've never found a partner I could be myself around."

Warm hands cup my cheeks, his thumbs swipe away the moisture pooling in my eyes. "I feel the same way, princess. I'm used to being the one in charge when it comes to sex. But with you, I feel safe enough to let myself be dominated. Does that make sense?"

I nod before turning and placing a kiss on his palm. "That's exactly how I feel, too, Cyrus. So I didn't take things too far?"

His chuckle has me smiling. "Definitely not. I'm up for round two if you are."

Eyes dipping down, I wince at the blood still dripping from his chest. It's going to stain my sheets for sure if I don't clean him up. The sex was definitely worth it, though. I have a feeling that's not the last time I'll be leaving marks on Cyrus. "I should probably bandage your chest. Did I hurt you?"

Cyrus's gaze drops to his chest, a frown pulling his mouth down at the corners. "Oh! I didn't even feel that. Guess I was too busy focusing on your tail in my ass." The sullen look on his face is soon replaced by a panty-melting crooked smirk.

I cackle as I stand from the bed and head to the bathroom. Flipping on the lights, I rummage through the cabinet until I find my first aid kit. Placing it on the counter, I clean myself up and wet a washcloth with warm, soapy water before leaving the bathroom.

By the time I get back to the bed, Cyrus's eyes are closed and his full lips are parted. A soft snore rumbles from his chest, and one corner of my mouth lifts into a small smile. "Sleeping beauty. Guess I really did drain you."

As gently as possible, so I don't wake him, I settle on the bed next to him and get to work cleaning and bandaging each cut.

As I work, my mind fills with images of this beautiful man in my bed every night. Images of Cyrus and I getting ready side by side every morning. Then working side by side every day.

The ultimate power couple of New York real estate.

I sigh, running my fingers through the dusting of dark-blonde hair on his chest. A girl can dream.

No matter how the presentation goes tomorrow, I have to tell him how I feel. Even if it's the most terrifying thing I've ever done in my life; I have to let him all the way into my heart if I want a future with him.

I have to say those three little words out loud.

CHAPTER 26

Cyrus

"And the second level would be converted into high-end housing with modern industrial architecture to bring in potential upscale buyers. The location right on the river is perfect for attracting clientele who want to venture out of the city, but don't want to live in the suburbs. It's the perfect mix of both worlds." Antoinette's heels clack against the tile floor as she paces in front of the conference table. Behind her, a three-dimensional rendering of the proposed warehouse renovations fills the projection screen.

From my seat at the end of the table, I can't take my eyes off her, totally enthralled by her confidence and charisma.

There's no way the board will turn down this proposal. She's a genius.

This morning when I woke up, Antoinette's armor was snuggly back in place. The strong, fearless creature I fell for was already dressed in a crisp black skirt and blazer, with her makeup done to perfection.

She was ready for battle.

You'd never know she was doubting herself mere hours before.

There's no trace of her dragon's temper as her glowing gaze sweeps over each board member's face.

There are four in total. Andrews and his elusive brother take up the seats in the center of the table, surrounded by their closest advisors. His assistant sits in the corner, typing furiously on his laptop.

Andrews's head bobs while Antoinette continues her presentation, but his thin lips are turned down in a grimace. The other board members share similar expressions, which send my stomach sinking like the Titanic.

"So, in conclusion, expanding our horizons outside the heart of the city would give Big York a new pool of potential clients and a new stream of revenue."

Standing from my seat, I walk to where Antoinette stands in the front of the room. Andrews and his cronies are too busy in a hushed discussion to pay us any attention, so I take the brief moment to squeeze Antoinette's hand in mine. Leaning in, my lips brush the shell of her ear when I speak. "You did amazing, princess."

Her cheeks darken to a lovely cherry shade, but a smile flits across her face. "Thank you," she whispers, eyes flicking to me before settling back on the men who quite literally decide our future at this company.

The chatter stops, and Andrews spins in his chair to face us. Clearing his throat, he rubs a hand over his shiny forehead. "This is what you've spent the past month working on?"

"Yes, sir," I answer. "Although I can't take much credit. Ms. Bauer is the brains behind this endeavor." I flash Antoinette what I hope is a reassuring smile.

"I see. And what makes you think Big York wants to expand into this type of endeavor?" His brow furrows, adding to his already grim appearance.

"The outskirts of the city are a completely untapped market, sir," Antoinette responds, hands clasped in front of her. "Big York could be the first company to breach the area, therefore reaping the most reward. You can't lose, sir." Her ruby-painted lips flit into a tight smile, but it doesn't reach her beautiful eyes.

"I see. And you felt you had the authority to make that call?" Andrews crosses his thick arms over his chest.

"I saw an opportunity and ran with it... sir." She forces the words out through gritted teeth. I'm surprised her fangs haven't splintered with how tight her jaw muscles are clenched.

"I see," Andrews hums. His brother leans close, whispering in his ear. "And Ms. Bauer was the spearhead for this project?"

"Yes, sir." Jumping in with my two cents, not that Antoinette needs rescuing by any means, I play on Andrews's and his brother's greedy nature. "Just think of all the money sitting in this area. There are more abandoned warehouses that we could renovate the same way... with your approval, of course."

"It's not about the money, Mr. Wilcox. It's about principle. Ms. Bauer has gone outside of her job description without approval. We didn't ask for you to come up with a new revenue stream. Stick to what you know."

"What?" Antoinette barks.

Andrews seems to ignore her. "Unfortunately, in light of the recent merger and internal audit, our budget only allows for one senior agent to remain on staff at this time. And, it seems, you've made our decision for us."

Blood pounds in my ears and nausea churns my stomach. This is what I was afraid of; they're going to fire one of us and I don't know what that means for us as a couple.

Antoinette has kept her cards close to her chest, and I have no idea if she's as head over heels as I am.

"What are you saying, sir?" Antoinette all but growls. When I glance her way, her hands are fisted at her sides and the beginnings of smoke curl from her nostrils.

Fuck it. In that moment, I don't care if the board finds out about us. All I care about is her. And I can't watch her spiral while I do nothing.

Shooting my hand out, I uncurl her fist and lace my fingers through hers. The skin is scorching to the touch, but I don't pull away. Let her burn me.

"I'm saying—" As Andrews continues, Antoinette's fingers curl tighter around my hand, to the point that tiny pricks of pain dance across the back of my hand. Her dragon is pushing to the surface, and her claws are out. "Ms. Bauer, your employment with Big York is terminated. Effective immediately. Security will follow you to your office, collect your belongings, and escort you from the building. Please do not cause a scene."

A clipped laugh bursts from her mouth when she yanks her hand from mine. "Good luck without me."

That's my girl.

I want to pump my fist in the air in a show of support... until her narrowed eyes slice from Andrews and his lackeys to *me*.

Head held high, her glowing gaze skims over me, like I'm no better than the dirt on her designer stilettos. "You're going to need it."

Wait, what? Does she think I knew this was coming? Is she lumping me in with *them*?

"Princess—"

"I knew it was too good to be true." Her lip pulls back into a snarl, one fang glinting in the harsh fluorescent lighting.

Before I can pick my jaw up off the floor, she tosses her hair over her shoulders and sashays toward the door, not giving any of us a backward glance.

A large man dressed in all black steps through the door and ushers Antoinette out of the room. The door slamming shut behind them is deafening in the silent conference room, and I'm torn between running after the woman I love and berating the man who broke her.

My boss stands from his chair and braces his hands on the wooden table. "Congratulations, Cyrus."

Narrowing my eyes, I approach them and straighten to my full height. "Do you know what you've done? You fired the wrong fucking person!" My voice rises as everything comes rushing to the surface. I need to get out of here and make sure Antoinette is okay. Hopefully, Pen intercepts her before she blows up the entire building.

The smile on Mr. Andrews's face falls.

"That woman is a loose cannon," his brother remarks. "She lets her emotions get the better of her too often. We've been looking for a reason to fire her for months now. Downsizing is the perfect excuse."

Fire licks at my veins as they all nod in agreement. "*That woman* is the best thing that's ever happened to me. This project." I sweep a hand behind me at the warehouse model. "This was all her idea. And it's fucking brilliant. Can't you see that?"

A chorus of grunts sound around me.

"If you think it's so great, then prove me wrong. I'll give you the budget to finish the project. But I assure you, there's no money there."

Are they fucking kidding? They're too stuck in their ways to see what Antoinette does. Expanding outside the city is the future of the industry.

"I can't believe this." My feet move without me noticing, pacing a path across the room and back as my brain scrambles to get a handle on the situation.

"Believe it, son. This is a huge advancement in your career. We're happy to have you as a permanent fixture on the Big York team. You can get rid of that airhead assistant, too. Find someone better suited for the job. In fact, my oldest son just graduated from college. He'd be a perfect addition to the team."

Of course, he'd boot a hardworking employee in favor of his own flesh and blood.

"There's been a misunderstanding. Antoinette Bauer is an invaluable part of this team, and if you can't see that, then you're dumber than you look." Should I be insulting my bosses? Probably not. But they hurt the woman I love.

"Watch it, Wilcox." Andrews stands, his chair rolling back with the force.

"I quit."

"What?" His face turns an alarming shade of red.

Stepping up to the table, I mirror his earlier stance and brace my hands on the smooth surface before glaring down my nose at them. "You heard me. *I quit.* If you can't see all the hard work Antoinette put into a project, that could be revolutionary for the future of this company, well, then I don't want to work here. She deserves all the credit, and you damn well know it. So I quit—effective immediately. You'll have my letter of resignation by the end of the day."

I've given these assholes too much of my time already. I should be with my dragon queen right now, comforting her and reassuring her that these idiots don't matter. She's better than this place.

Ignoring their shouts behind me, I push through the door and race toward the stairwell that will take me to Antoinette.

CHAPTER 27

Antoinette

My whole body burns, like I'm going to combust at any second. Black plumes of smoke billow from my nostrils, leaving a trail behind me as I pace in front of the windows.

"How could he!?" The growled words claw from my voice box, broken and harsh. My dragon tears her way through my skin until my nails lengthen into sharp claws, and scales line my arms.

A shrill alarm filters through my raging thoughts of Cyrus's betrayal, but I don't care. Not even when the sprinklers on the ceiling kick on, dousing me in their chilling spray. The water simply sizzles against any exposed flesh, evaporating into thin air.

It's too late. I'm lost in the anger as it takes over my body.

Did Cyrus know they were planning to fire me all along? Is that why he agreed so easily to work with me in the first place?

And Andrews—sniveling asshole!

"Do something!" Pen's pleading voice is garbled, like I'm underwater. Like I'm drowning. I don't know who she's talking to, and I don't care.

My vision flickers, everything tinted in an ugly red haze. Sweeping an arm across my desk, I send the singed remains of my potted plant and coffee mug flying. Ceramic shards, dirt, and leaves spray across the floor as they shatter onto the hard tile.

My chest burns as the organ inside splinters into a million pieces. He fucking betrayed me again. The bastard.

Water continues to spill down like rain, but it does nothing to extinguish my rage.

Heavy hands clasp onto my shoulders, halting my clipped steps. I'm spun until I'm facing a wall of muscle encased in the finest designer suit.

"You!" I snarl, poking a claw into his hard chest. "I let you in, and you fucking broke me!"

Tears stream from my eyes, evaporating against my skin before they can even fall to the ground. It's like I'm on fire, and I don't know how to stop it. I've never been this consumed by my dragon's rage before.

"Antoinette. Please. It's not what you're thinking." Cyrus's hands cup my face, but he hisses, pulling away like he's been burned.

Smoke continues to swirl around us, mixing with the falling water. The shrill cry of the fire alarm finally stops. The only sound in the room is the pounding of water from the sprinklers and my panted breaths.

"Princess, look at me." His voice is more commanding this time. Hands back on my face, he tips my chin up until I meet his gaze.

The pain in his icy-blue eyes douses the inferno in my veins until my claws retract and the smoke clears.

"I quit, princess," he says, leaning his forehead against mine.

My belly swoops. "W-Why would you do that?"

A ghosted breath fans my face when he huffs a laugh. "Infuriating, strong woman. Don't you see?"

I shake my head. Tears burn my eyes.

"Fuck those assholes. If they can't see how amazing and brilliant you are, then I don't want to work here either. If anything, I'm the one who deserves to be fired."

I hiccup as his words sink in. He didn't betray me. The fist around my heart loosens. "But—"

Soft lips land on mine, silencing my protest. "Listen to me, princess. I would do anything for you." Truth shines in his eyes, mixed with an emotion that still terrifies me a little. *Love.* "I would burn down the whole fucking city if you asked me to. Even though that's more your territory." He chuckles, fingers skimming a path over my cheekbone to my hair, where he brushes a damp strand behind my ear. "You're my partner. My person. My family." His gaze softens, along with his deep voice. "You're it for me, princess. I love you."

"You-You—" I think he broke my brain. The logical part of me can't compute another being caring for me so deeply.

"You heard me, Bauer. I fucking love you. You don't have to say it back right now. I know you're not used to letting people in, but I need you to know that I'm not going anywhere." Lifting his head, he sweeps his eyes around us. Probably taking in the utter chaos I've caused. "Jobless, soaked to the bone, smelling like a bonfire, I'm in this with you. Okay?"

All I can do is nod. His confession has left me reeling for words, yet oddly content at the same time. He's not leaving me. He didn't throw me under the bus and take my job.

"But we should probably get out of here before Andrews calls the cops, and we get arrested."

When Cyrus pulls away, spinning toward the door, my brain finally catches up. Balling the back of his jacket in my fist, I tug until he stumbles backward, nearly knocking me to the floor in the process.

"What—" He turns to face me, and I rise onto my tip-toes, slamming my mouth against his.

With a groan, he melts into me, wrapping his arms around me and tugging me to his chest.

Drenched clothes stick to my heated skin, but I don't care. I attack his lips with mine, taking what I've been yearning to have my whole life. "I love you, too, Cyrus," I gasp between desperate kisses.

Finally speaking those words out loud is big and scary. So fucking scary, but I trust Cyrus with my heart.

I clasp his face between my hands, relishing the familiar rasp of his five o'clock shadow as his dark vanilla scent floods all of my senses. In his arms, I'm finally home after a lifetime of being alone.

"Hey, Annie..." As much as I don't want to, the urgent tone in Pen's voice has me ripping away from the kiss.

Pen's eyes widen, her head turned toward the hallway, where a fuming Andrews marches toward us. The rest of the board members trail behind him. "You might want to get out of here before he calls the police. I'll try to hold them off." With a wink, she sprints out of the office, intercepting our boss.

Swiping my soggy tote bag from my desk, I kick off my heels before gripping Cyrus's hand and pulling him toward the door.

"Wait! Where are we going?" There's confusion in his voice, but his footsteps follow mine as my bare feet slap against the wet tile.

"The roof!" Slamming the door open to the stairwell, I tug him behind me and race up the stairs.

My body sings with excitement when I push through the door to the roof, the midday sun beating down from above to warm my slick skin. This is the start of something new and exciting. No more chauvinistic boss to worry about. No more working myself to the bone for someone else.

I don't have enough money to start my own firm yet, but I'm nothing if not resourceful. I'll think of something.

Getting fired was the final push I needed to finally reach for my dream. I suppose I should send Andrews a thank-you card once I'm the top firm in the city.

Turning toward Cyrus, I walk backward to the middle of the roof. My fingers find the buttons on my singed blouse, hurriedly working the damp fabric from my body as my dragon swells within me. "We're free, Cyrus. We can do whatever the fuck we want. And right now, I want to take you for a ride."

Throwing him a saucy wink, I peel my soaked bra from my body.

Cyrus saunters toward me, tucking his hands in his pockets. "As much as I'd love to try exhibitionism with you, princess, getting arrested wasn't on my calendar for today."

Laughing, I shove his chest. "Not what I meant, Wilcox. Let me fly you to my favorite spot, then we'll go back to my place."

"Sounds like a plan."

Tossing my sodden skirt and panties to the side, I let my dragon free. Flames burst from my skin and scales sprout across my body. Wings and tail unravel as I grow and morph, the transformation taking hold.

Extending my wings, I crane my neck to the side and find Cyrus. With a slack jaw, his heated gaze travels every inch of scales and claws. "I'm never going to get used to how beautiful you are," he murmurs, stepping closer to brush a hand over the rippling black and gold scales. "In every form."

My body shudders under his gentle caress and heartfelt words, but a pounding at the roof access door has me dipping down and meeting him with an expectant tip of my head.

"You want me to ride on your back?" His throat bobs and his eyebrows dip.

I snort, crouching lower to the ground.

Finally getting with the program, Cyrus climbs onto my broad back, straddling the base of my neck, right above my wings. The security guards break through the door as my feet spring from the gravel and we jolt into the clear blue sky.

CHAPTER 28

Cyrus

A shiver rushes through my body as the cool air brushes my damp clothes. "This is fucking amazing!" I shout over the breeze, but I don't know if Antoinette can even hear me.

I'm riding a dragon! Walking into our office earlier, I thought Antoinette was going to burn the entire building to the ground. Pen was frantic, chasing after her with a fire extinguisher. But it's like her usual soothing words bounced right off Antoinette's armor.

Until I showed up. One look into those molten golden eyes and she seemed to cool immediately.

And when she said she loves me, I think my heart nearly exploded at hearing those sweet words from her lips.

For a second, I almost thought she was going to blame me for getting fired, but she surprised me, taking comfort in my presence when she used to shut me out.

The wind whistles by my ears, and I bend until my face is closer to the side of hers. "Where are we going?" I yell over the flapping of her wings and the air racing past us.

Instead of answering me, Antoinette tilts her body, forcing me to grip her neck tighter when we veer left. Like I'm on a rollercoaster, my stomach swoops with the sudden drop, but I feel weightless. It's amazing!

Down below, blinding light dances off the surface of the water, sparkling like diamonds with every wave and ripple. Antoinette flaps her wings slower, gliding on the breeze as we approach... "Is that the Statue of Liberty?"

Recognizable by the distinct green patina of the spiked crown and torch, Antoinette circles the statue with grace and ease, in total control in her dragon form. I'm in awe. This powerful creature has been hiding in the same office as me all this time.

Sure, I saw her during our game of chase at Maggie's orchard, but it was dark, and I was too drunk on the lust flowing through my veins.

Right now, my head is clear and there's not a cloud in the sky.

My hands run up the sides of her scale-covered neck, smooth and warm; the sunlight plays on each scale, making them sparkle like the rarest of black opals.

Her wings brush my legs with each flap, and I curl my feet tighter to her body while turning to admire the webbed membrane. Just like the other night, it reminds me of a galaxy. Swirling specs of black, gold, and navy weave together to create a beautiful masterpiece that glitters in the sun.

I'm so lost in my perusal of Antoinette, I don't notice we're back at her penthouse until her giant clawed feet touch down on the balcony. Stumbling, I scramble from her back and nearly land on my ass as she bursts into flames. A naked, human Antoinette stands before me not even a second later.

Before I can get a single word out, her hands are in my hair and her lips are on mine. The kiss is desperate, a claiming in some ways. My hands find the supple flesh of her ass, boosting her up until she wraps her luscious thighs around my waist.

My clothes are dried from the ride here, but her hands pull and rip until my jacket, tie, and shirt flutter to the ground.

Greedy hands run over the muscles of my chest and back as she continues to attack my mouth with hers. Somehow, I stumble into her bedroom, and we land on her bed in a tangle of limbs.

She's panting when she pulls her mouth from mine. "I want to mate you. Will you let me?" Flames flicker in her eyes as she stares up at me.

"What does that mean? Mate me?" My eyebrows dip. If it means being with her for the rest of my life, then I'm one hundred percent in.

Her slender fingers stroke my hair in a soothing, hypnotic pattern, and I lean further into her touch. Lately, she's more willing to show affection, and I lap that shit up, bathing in her gentle caresses and freely given kisses.

"It's extremely rare. A legend my mother told me when I was small," she says, voice rich and alluring. "But every once in a while, a dragon finds a partner they want to spend eternity with. A mate."

"Your parents. Were they mates?"

She shakes her head, eyes closing as she swallows. When her eyes open again, there's a hint of sadness in them. "No, they weren't mates. And, maybe, that's why my dad didn't stick around. I'll never know."

Bracing on one hand, I cup her cheek with the other. Opalescent black scales burst through the skin, something she's also been doing more around me—letting glimpses of her beautiful dragon out more often. I love seeing the real Antoinette. My thumb sweeps over her cheekbone, and I savor the rough texture of each scale. The warmth like a burst of sunshine shooting straight to my skittering heart. "You know I'd never leave you, right?"

She nods, fingers still weaving through my hair, like she can't bear to let me go. Her other hand presses on my chest, forcing me to lie on the bed next to her. "And I'd never leave you. When I'm with you, I'm whole for the first time in my life. I don't have this empty pit in my heart anymore. All thanks to you, Cyrus."

"Ditto, princess. So what does mating entail?" I smile at the word—*mate*. It's different, but I don't hate it. Especially if it means I'm hers.

"According to legend, it has to happen during sex."

My eyes dip down to her full breasts. The rosy nipples harden under my scrutinizing gaze, and I lick my lips. "I'm game." Reaching out, I flick the tight bead of flesh.

Her chest shakes with a husky laugh, causing her breasts to bounce... and my cock to harden. "I'm serious, Cyrus."

"So am I." I swing my gaze back to hers, only to find lust replacing any previous emotion.

Huffing a breath, she continues. "I'm immortal, so if we're going to be together, we need to solidify our mate bond with a bite."

"Kinky." I wink at her, but she rolls her eyes.

"This is serious, Wilcox! If I bite you, it will sync up our life spans. You'll be immortal, Cyrus. It's not reversible, so you have to be absolutely sure." She pauses, searching my face. "Are you sure you want to be stuck with me forever? I'm moody and bossy and a workaholic. I don't like being told what to do, and I'm not the best at letting people in."

My thumb brushes under her eye, catching a lone tear before it can fall. Living forever with this smart, stubborn, gorgeous creature by my side sounds like fucking heaven. "Trust me, princess. If I can't handle you at your worst, do I really deserve to be with you at your best? You're not going to scare me off now. I'm in too deep. I'm all the way in, if you are."

Her head bobs, a radiant smile on her face, and her eyes shimmering. "Yes. I'm so far in that it terrifies me sometimes. But I love you, Cyrus."

Those words pull a groan from my chest before I slam my mouth to hers, continuing our earlier heated kiss.

Rolling her to the center of the bed, I nestle between her spread thighs, the heat of her cunt calling to my throbbing cock. The hard length presses against my zipper, nearly boring a hole in the fabric to get inside my sweet dragon. "So how's this gonna work, princess? I fuck you and you bite me." My lips trail down her neck as I speak, the words heating her already burning skin. I love how she's always so warm, welcoming my touch... and my cock.

Her laughter rings through the air. The sound is more free than ever. "Remember when I said I don't like being told what to do?"

Before I can respond, I'm pinned to the bed, an utterly feral Antoinette straddling my hips. Beams of sunlight stream through the windows behind the bed, illuminating her spread wings and fiery eyes. The flick of her tail behind her back catches my eyes, anticipation roaring to life in my veins as my cock leaks in my pants.

Trailing her hands down my stomach, I suck in a breath. Antoinette quickly unbuckles my belt. Undoing the button and zipper, she tugs my pants and boxers down, leaving me totally naked and exposed under her penetrating stare.

On cue, my cock jumps against my stomach, hard and ready.

She must notice because she circles her claw-tipped fingers around my shaft, squeezing until I groan, and twisting her wrist as she strokes me. "I want you delirious with pleasure and begging for my bite before I sink my teeth into your skin, Cyrus. Can you do that for me?"

"Yes, princess. Yes." My words fade off on a moan when she twists her wrist again, applying the perfect amount of pressure to send a trickle of pre-cum rushing from the tip of my cock.

She could ask me to jump off a cliff right now, and I'd happily take the plunge.

This beautiful woman has my whole soul, and I never want it back.

I want her to keep me for eternity.

"Keep moving your hand like that, and I'll be begging in no time," I rasp.

When she leans down, forked tongue skating up the sides of my shaft, all the breath leaves my lungs on a choked moan. I'm light-headed, every last drop of blood pulsing to my cock, the flesh red and angry.

"Please, princess."

Reaching the tip, she moans and laps up the bead of pre-cum. "You taste so good, my love. Give me more."

Then her lips wrap around my shaft and she slides her mouth all the way down until her nose brushes my pelvis. The muscles in her throat contract around my weeping cock, forcing another rush of pre-cum. Antoinette moans again, the sound vibrating straight to my balls, and I almost lose my load right then and there.

Gagging slightly, she pulls back with a gasp, my cock slipping from her sinful mouth. Before she can dive back down, I weave my fingers through her hair, holding her steady so we're eye to eye. "If you do that again, I'm gonna come. And I don't want to waste a drop in your perfect mouth, Antoinette. I only come in your cunt right now. Got it?"

Defiance flares in her eyes, but her puffy lips pull into a smirk, exposing sharp fangs. "You're not doing very well at this whole begging thing, Wilcox."

That fucking does it. Wrapping my fingers around her hips, they dig into the soft cushion of fat when I drag her up my body. She squeaks a protest, but comes willingly.

Once we're face to face, her breath fanning my lips, I say, "Please, princess. Let me fill your beautiful cunt with all of my cum for the rest of eternity. Take pity on your mate, my beautiful dragon queen. Let him breed you over and over until you can't possibly take another drop." I hold her gaze, rocking her against my cock. "Is that good enough for you, Bauer?"

Humor dances across her features, a laugh puffing against my lips. "I suppose that will do."

She straightens and rises onto her knees, wings flapping lazily behind her as she wraps a hand around my shaft and lines the tip up to her opening. "You're sure?" A hint of doubt breaks through the lust on her face, and I hate it. I never want her to doubt my love for her. Ever.

"I am one thousand percent sure, Antoinette. You don't like being told what to do—well, I don't do anything I don't want to. I love you, and I want to spend the rest of my life showing you how much you mean to me."

Any hesitation fades from her beautiful face, the strong and stunning dragon breaking through.

I groan and tighten my hands around her hips when she slips the tip of my cock into her ribbed cunt. The tight walls flutter, loosening as she sinks all the way down to the base with a swivel of her hips. I'm hypnotized by the sway of her plump breasts and the swell of her stomach while she rides my cock. There's no way I'm going to last long when this sex goddess is on top of me.

Tipping her head back, her wings open to their full span, and she moans. "Cyrus, yes. You feel so good inside me. I never want this to end.""It doesn't have to,"

I promise on a groan, grinding my hips up so her clit drags against me. The smooth, scaled flesh of her tail slides around my leg, twining tight, like she's anchoring me to her in every way.

I like that. Knowing she needs to be surrounded by me just as much as I need to be surrounded by her.

"So good, Cyrus," she moans, working her hips in a frenzy, chasing the high we both need.

Reaching a hand around her back, I grip the base of her tail—right above the crack of her perfect ass—guiding her to ride me harder. Faster.

My other hand grips the supple flesh of her ass cheek, fingers digging in as I pump my hips, fucking her from below.

Suddenly, her hands slap against my chest, eyes glowing like lava, brighter than ever before. Black scales creep along her hairline and cheekbones, lining the perimeter of her face before disappearing down her neck. They extend from her claw-tipped fingers, which dig into my pec muscles, up to her elbows.

Her body is more scales than skin at this point, and she's fucking stunning.

"I'm gonna come. Bite me now, princess. It has to be now!" I'm not sure how I know this. Some foreign instinct takes over, and the need for her fangs in my neck hums in my blood.

Dipping down, Antoinette obliges, running her nose up the side of my neck, like she's scenting me. At the first prick on her sharp teeth, her pussy muscles clamp around my cock, almost to the point of pain.

But the discomfort turns to euphoria when her fangs sink into my neck. It's like every ounce of tension rushes from my body until I'm floating on a cloud.

White spots dance across my vision, and I slam my eyes shut. My cock jolts, spurting cum into her womb while I moan.

Antoinette moans against my neck, her tight pussy locking around me as she succumbs to her orgasm.

When I open my eyes, we're surrounded by glowing golden flames. "H-holy shit," I whisper, lifting my hand from her hip to reach toward the flickering wall of fire rising from the bed. My fingers sift through it, and rather than being burned, a cooling sensation washes over me. "Antoinette, look."

Retracting her fangs, the hot sweep of her tongue laps at the blood trickling from the wound. "Mmmm, what?" Her head lifts, eyes widening as she takes in the strange inferno surrounding us. Scaled fingers thread through mine, turning our hands this way and that as the flames dance around us. "This must be the mate bond cementing."

"How long does it last?"

Dark eyebrows pinch. "I'm not sure. Do you feel any different?" Her head tilts from the fire to me.

I shrug, wiggling my toes and fingers, twisting my head. "No?" Then my cock twitches inside her cunt, an electric jolt of pleasure shooting down my spine. "Wait."

Gripping her hips again, I give a testing thrust. Yep, definitely hard again.

She squeals, but it turns to laughter when I roll us and settle on top of her. Fuck, she's beautiful. Messy raven hair spilling around her like a dark waterfall. Iridescent scales gleaming in the sunlight. And the most striking thing of all: her golden gaze that ensnared me from the first moment we were forced to share an office.

Bending my neck, I kiss her. Unhurried. Lazy strokes of my tongue against hers.

"Do dragons not have a refractory period?" I ask, slowly thrusting into her.

She pulls away from my lips, but I chase her, kissing down her neck as I make love to my mate. "I don't know. I've never had sex with a dragon. Maybe immortal males don't?"

I growl, sucking her hard nipple into my mouth. "Doesn't matter," I mumble around a mouthful of her heated flesh. "I'll just have to fuck you over and over and over again. Fill you with so much cum, it's leaking from your pores."

Arching her neck, she moans when I latch my teeth around her nipple and tug. "Yes."

This round is different from her earlier claiming. We take our time. Hands caressing scales and skin. Lips no longer desperate, but reverent.

We reach the peak together, a symphony of moans as I hold her tight, taking comfort in the warmth of her body. This is what the rest of my life will be like. A long and happy one, with Antoinette by my side.

Once we're finished, finally boneless and satiated, a small line of smoke trails from Antoinette's mouth. Fingers pinched like she's holding a cigarette, she swings her eyes toward me. "Are you ready for round three?"

"Very funny." I tuck an arm behind my head, lying on my back next to her in her ridiculously soft bed. "Give me a couple minutes."

She laughs, but her face falls, all joking aside when her expression sobers. "In all seriousness. What are we going to do now? We're jobless in New York City. This apartment isn't cheap. But I don't think Andrews will give either of us a glowing review after what happened today." She winces, no doubt remembering the utter chaos we left behind for poor Penelope to deal with.

We should probably call and check on her.

"You know," I say, wrapping an arm around her and tugging her against my chest—where she belongs. "O'Malley never signed the warehouse over to Big York. And he did say it was meant to be *yours*." I stroke a hand over my chin, a plan forming in my mind. "I have a pretty good chunk in savings."

Her eyebrows rise. "So do I. I was only working for Andrews to make enough to start my own firm."

Hope flickers like a flame between us. "What if I became your investor? If we pool our money, I bet we'd have enough for you to start your own firm. What do you say, princess? Wanna be my boss?"

"I thought you'd never ask."

EPILOGUE

Antoinette

A Few Months Later

T he keys jingle as Mr. O'Malley places them in my palm. He curls my fingers around the cool metal and cups my hand between both of his. "This place is finally gettin' the attention it deserves. All thanks ta you, lassie." One thick white eyebrow dips as he winks.

After his conversation with Cyrus, Mr. O'Malley never signed the contract with Big York. Something about his gut telling him it wasn't the right fit. He gladly signed the abandoned warehouse over to me when we told him what happened. Now I get to build the property of my dreams—on my own terms.

As far as Big York? We didn't exactly part on good terms. They didn't press charges for the destruction caused by the fire and water from the sprinkler system. Although, I did have to shell out a pretty penny for repairs.

It was a small price to pay to finally be my own boss and have the partner of my dreams by my side.

They did fire Penelope for being an "accomplice" to my vandalism. But she's tagging along on this new adventure with Cyrus and me.

This warehouse will be the birthplace of Bauer Enterprises. *My* company.

The old man gives my hand a gentle squeeze before releasing me and taking a step back. "And I see ye whipped this one into shape?"

A warm hand sliding around my back, and landing on my hip, has my mouth splitting into a smile.

"She sure did." Cyrus's deep voice vibrates through me. I close my eyes, soaking up every drop like a spring rain on parched earth.

"I'll get outta yer hair then. I can't wait to see what ye do with this old girl." With a final wink, Mr. O'Malley shuffles outside, the heavy metal door slamming behind him, and leaving Cyrus and me in silence.

I turn in a circle, stilettos crunching on some loose concrete, and images of this place in a year or two flashing in my head. The exposed beams paying homage to the original structure. Large banks of windows letting in every beam of daylight possible.

"You know..." Cyrus's voice interrupts my daydreams, and I spin toward the door. The lock clicks into place, and I can guarantee he has something naughty in mind. "I've had a little fantasy in mind since our night at the orchard."

"Oh? Another one?"

His shiny leather loafers click against the cement floor as he prowls around me in a slow circle. Stalking me like an apex predator.

At a torturous pace, he makes his way to my back, hard chest brushing against me when he heaves a breath. "Yes, princess. We have eternity to explore our fantasies. So why don't we get started?"

I shiver at the promise in his dark tone.

"Now, be a good little dragon... and run."

Behind my ribcage, my heart kicks into high gear, anticipation and lust overtaking my body. Peering over my shoulder, Cyrus's pale eyes burn with the same cocktail of emotions thrumming through my veins.

Dipping my chin, my gaze snags on the silver crescent scars on his neck. My mark.

Every time I see it, my body ignites with an inferno. The need to claim him in my half-dragon form roaring to life.

"You're not making this a very interesting chase, Bauer." His plush lips curl into a cocky grin.

"Fuck you, Wilcox," I spit, but there's no venom behind my words. In truth, I love this game of cat and mouse just as much as he does.

Would I prefer to be the one doing the chasing? Yes.

But beggars can't be choosers.

Either way, I'm sure an orgasm or two is in my near future.

"Oh, I plan on it, princess." An open palm connects with my ass cheek. Pain jolts me forward as the sting of his slap soaks through my pencil skirt. "Now get your fine ass moving."

So I kick my red-bottom heels off, giving him a significant height advantage over me. Although, I have something he doesn't—my scales ripple across my skin as my dragon makes her presence in this game known.

I take off at a full sprint into the empty warehouse, bare feet slapping against the cold concrete floor as I dodge old palettes and fallen chunks of the roof. "Catch me if you can, Wilcox!" Lost to the expansive space, my voice echoes into the darkness.

Most of the overhead lights are broken, bathing the warehouse in shadows. Perfect for evading my mate and hiding.

Slipping behind an old stack of shipping crates, I lean against the rough wood to catch my breath. Even as an immortal, Cyrus doesn't have the same supernatural senses I do, so I doubt his ears can detect my hoarse panted breaths.

"Come out, come out, wherever you are!" His baritone voice rings with the promise of what's to come.

Much like me, Cyrus's sexual appetite requires both rough, hard fucking and slow, sensual lovemaking.

We really are made for each other.

"Little dragon," he calls again. This time his voice is closer, on the other side of the boxes I'm hidden behind.

Heart hammering, I take off again.

"Found you!" His shoes echo behind me as he gives chase.

Shit!

Just as I think I've evaded him, a hand snags in the back of my hair, pain shooting through my scalp and stopping me dead in my tracks with a strangled cry.

Using his grip, he slams me back into his hard chest. Warmth seeps through my thin silk blouse. He must have taken off his shirt. I try to turn and catch a glimpse of his toned pecs, dusted with a thatch of golden hair that calls to my fingers. They twitch at my sides with the need to touch him. My mate.

But Cyrus has other plans. Holding my head tight, he restricts my movement and marches me toward the outer wall of the warehouse, the smooth concrete towering in front of us. "Eyes forward, hands on the wall."

I squeak at the gritted command in his voice, helpless to do anything but obey.

Over time, it's gotten easier for me to slip into a more submissive role with Cyrus. He's shown me I can trust him wholeheartedly, especially with my vulnerability.

Hands smacking against the cool wall, I shiver when his fingers slip to the zipper at the back of my skirt. This possessive side of Cyrus is just as much my favorite as when he obeys my every command like a good boy.

Uncurling his fingers from my hair, two rough palms slip under the waist of my skirt, pushing it down until it pools at my feet, leaving me in my sleeveless blouse and lace thong. "So fucking beautiful," he growls, hands running up my outer thighs to cup each mound of my ass.

His touch brushes under the loose silk of my shirt, coasting over the extra fat of my stomach.

I've never felt more beautiful than when his hands are running over every inch of my body and his eyes are memorizing each dip and curve. "What did I do in a past life to deserve to spend forever with you, my beautiful dragon queen?" Forehead resting on my shoulder, his hands tease higher, dipping into the cups of my bra to tweak my nipples.

Lost to the sensation of his breath on my neck and his hands on my breasts, I moan, pushing my hips back to rub against the erection tenting his pants. "Please, Cyrus. I need you inside me."

He growls, rolling his forehead against my shoulder. "Fuck, I love when you beg. Do it again."

He trails kisses up the side of my neck, and I tip my head back, giving him more room. "Please, mate. I need your cock inside me, filling me until I don't know where I end and you start. Fuck me so deep and so hard that I can taste every drop of your cum." As I give in and beg, Cyrus works the buttons loose on my shirt. Lowering my arms, the silky fabric slips from my shoulders to join my discarded skirt on the ground.

Wasting no time, he unhooks the clasp of my bra. My breasts spring free when he peels the lacy garment from my body.

Once my chest is bare to him, I immediately slap my hands where they belong: against the cool concrete in front of me.

"Good girl. You beg so prettily for your mate." Goosebumps spread across my skin at his praise. My nipples harden to painful peaks when he cups my breasts, squeezing them together with a groan.

I might love to be in charge, but Cyrus's words of adoration nearly bring me to my knees.

Standing in front of him in nothing but my thong, he towers over me, sliding his hands over every inch of my body with the promise of every wicked thing he has planned. "If I dip my fingers into your panties, will you be dripping for me, princess?"

I whimper, nodding like a damn bobble-head doll. My cunt pulses when his fingers run down my stomach, dipping into my belly button before toying with the waistband of my panties. Pressing my hips forward, I chase his touch, needing those thick fingers stretching me where it aches most.

His dark chuckle wafts against the shell of my ear. "Are you needy, Antoinette?"

"Yes!" The word turns into a cry of ecstasy as his fingers finally snake into my panties, plunging deep into my soaked core.

God, he feels so good.

His thumb circles my clit. Taunting. Teasing. While his fingers stretch and curl.

The force of each thrust causes me to rise onto my toes, hands skating further up the wall. "You're so tight. I can't wait to get my cock in you, princess."

Pleasure coils low in my belly. "Please, Cyrus. Make me come."

And he does. Thumb pressing against my sensitive clit, he curls his fingers one last time against my G-spot, and I detonate. Legs shaking, chest heaving, I collapse forward, but Cyrus wraps an arm around my waist to support me.

"Good girl. Now you're ready for my cock." In the haze of my orgasm, the clink of his belt buckle and the snick of his zipper being lowered are almost drowned out by my harsh breaths. Canting my hips back with his hands, he pulls my thong to the side and nudges the fat tip of his cock against my entrance.

Cyrus might still be human—although an immortal one—but the man's cock is pure magic. I'm never left unsatisfied. Usually orgasming twice before he fills me with his release.

I press back, my pussy swallowing the tip of his cock, and we both groan. "That's it, princess. Wish you could see the way your pretty cunt stretches to take my cock. I've never seen anything quite so perfect."

Fingers digging into my hips, there's a bite of pain from his nails, but it has me sighing and meeting his thrusts as he fills me to the limit. "So good, Cyrus. Don't stop."

"I know, princess. I feel it, too." Hands never leaving my hips, he pounds into me, hot breaths fanning across the base of my neck.

One hand leaves my hip, and I whimper at the loss of his touch, the skin growing cold. But Cyrus runs that hand up my spine until it's fisted in the back of my hair. Tangling into the dark waves, he tilts my head until I'm met by his glacial-blue stare.

Mouth falling slack, I drown in the liquid ocean of his eyes while he continues to work me closer to another orgasm. Lips hovering over mine, he whispers, "I love you, Antoinette."

I smile, then nip my teeth into his lower lip before plunging my tongue into the wet heat of his mouth.

Breaking the kiss, I murmur, "I love you, Cyrus. Thank you for breaking down my walls." Then my lips are back on his, both of us rocketing into euphoria as his hips stutter, filling me with his cum.

Cyrus

Untangling my fingers from her messy hair, I wrap both arms around Antoinette. She sags forward, letting me support her weight.

Over the last few months, she's gotten better at asking for help and telling me when she's overwhelmed. It doesn't mean she's weak, which is something I have to remind her of constantly.

On the contrary, this beautiful creature clutched in my arms is one of the strongest women I've ever met.

She took being fired as a motivator, and I predict Bauer Enterprises will be one of the top earning property brokers in the city. Give her time, and Antoinette will blow them all out of the water. I'll happily stand by her side as she builds her empire.

The ribbed walls of her pussy flutter, unlocking from my cock, but I'm still rock hard. One of the lovely side effects of our mate bond is my insatiable appetite for Antoinette. So it's a good thing we work for ourselves now and can sneak off for a midday quickie... or two.

"Don't move," I command, slipping from her heat to kneel behind her.

As I descend, I tug her thong down her legs, letting the ruined lace pool at her feet.

My hands glide over the soft, dimpled flesh of her ass—one of my favorite parts of her.

Not to be outshined by her beautiful heart, obviously.

Thumbs running the crease of her ass, I spread her cheeks until her glistening pussy is exposed. It's pink and puffy, filled to the brim.

"What are you doing back there?" She tilts her head, probably trying to get a good look behind her.

The slap echoes through the empty warehouse when my hand collides with the side of her ass cheek. "Eyes forward, hands on the wall. Let a man admire his handiwork in peace."

She widens her stance, tipping her hips up until a trail of milky white cream drips from her stuffed pussy. Still coated in our releases, my cock jerks between my legs, ready for round two.

I growl, running my fingers through the mess between her legs before plunging two inside her entrance. "So warm and wet for me."

"Always you. *Only* you, Cyrus."

Fuck, I need her again.

Straightening to my full height, I bring my lips to her ear, voice a husky whisper. "Shift for me, princess. Show me your dragon."

Eyes blazing, she spins to face me, but scales scatter across her skin, gleaming in the low light spilling through the holes in the ceiling.

Wings sprout from her shoulder blades as I back her against the wall, using my height to my advantage.

"You're already hard again?" A single black eyebrow rises on her face, but her lips curve into a smirk that showcases her sharp teeth.

Hooking my arms under her legs, I scoop her up. She's forced to wrap her strong, luscious thighs around my waist. "I'm always hard for you, princess. Now and for eternity. You're my queen."

Not wasting another second, I plunge my cock back into her heat, fucking her hard and fast until she's screaming my name. It's music to my ears as it echoes through the expansive space, filling my heart to the brim.

Balls drawing up tight, I take her mouth with mine and let her swallow my moans, emptying my load into her womb.

My chest heaves and my legs wobble, so I slide down to the floor with my spent cock still sheathed inside Antoinette. She nuzzles against the side of my neck, and I stroke my fingers through the soft strands of her hair while I catch my breath.

"I think we've sufficiently christened the place. What do you think?"

I can't stop the chuckle that rumbles out of my mouth, joined by Antoinette's melodic laughter. "Yeah, princess, I think so, too. We'll have to come back for another round once the remodel is done."

Twinkling golden eyes meet mine when she lifts her head. Flushed cheeks and tousled hair making her even more beautiful. Her tail tightens around my waist, holding us closer together. "You're on, Wilcox."

I thought I lost my chance at a happily ever after when my husband died, but maybe I was wrong.

Curious about Cyrus's sister-in-law, Maggie Wilcox? Stay tuned for a steamy opposites attract monster romance featuring a single mom and the vampire nanny Cyrus hires for the summer.

The Vampire in the Orchard is next in the Monstrous New York universe!

E.M. SAUBER
paranormal
romance author

E.M. Sauber was born and raised in the Midwest. Reading has always been a part of her life. A way to escape when the real world gets to be too much.

She currently lives in Minnesota with her wonderful husband, two children, and two dogs.

When she isn't writing steamy shifter stories, you can find her cuddled on the couch under a fuzzy blanket with her kindle or daydreaming about a new idea for a book.